THE BEVERLY GRAY MYSTERY STORIES

BEVERLY GRAY'S SECRET

The BEVERLY GRAY *Mystery Stories*

By CLAIR BLANK

"Run!" Larry whispered, giving Beverly a push

Beverly Gray's Secret

BEVERLY GRAY'S SECRET

By CLAIR BLANK

GROSSET & DUNLAP

Publishers   NEW YORK

Printed in the United States of America

Contents

Contents

BEVERLY GRAY'S SECRET

CHAPTER I

Bad News

"STOP pacing up and down, Bev!" Lenora White-hill entreated. "You'll wear out the rug."

"Let her pace," Shirley Parker said. "It's *her* job she's worrying about."

"It's my job, too," Lenora reminded her friend. "Because where Beverly goes, I go. Not even editor Charlie Blaine can break up our team."

"You are an unbeatable reporter-and-photographer combination," Lois Mason assured Lenora, smiling, "and it's much too early in the morning to think about such things as losing your job. Let's talk about something more pleasant. Where shall the *Susabella* dock next?"

For weeks, the four girls, together with Miss Ernwood their chaperon, Roger Garrett, Shirley's fiancé, and owner and captain of the yacht, Larry Owens, who was engaged to Beverly, Terry Cartwright, and Jim Stanton had cruised Pacific waters, calling at popular as well as out-of-the-way ports, acquiring health, suntan, and a host of never-to-be-forgotten memories.

"I'd like to go to South America," blonde Lenora announced firmly as she swung a pair of pajama-clad legs over the side of her bunk. "I know we've been there before, but we didn't have time to see half of all the interesting things there are to see."

"I'd like that, too," Lois agreed from the opposite side of the room. "How about you, Shirley?"

"I think it would be fine." Shirley ruffled her red hair and appealed to the fourth girl. "What do you say, Bev?"

A slender, auburn-haired girl turned from the porthole through which she had been watching majestic Diamond Head looming up in the distance.

"I'd love it," Beverly declared. "It will make a good finale to our trip."

"And after South America we will have to go home," Lois sighed. "I wonder if things are just the same in New York as they were when we left?'' she added.

Four reminiscent smiles broke forth as each girl thought of the pleasant apartment they shared together in New York and the life they led there.

Lois was on the staff of a fashion magazine and she felt a thrill of anticipation when she thought of the new ideas she had garnered on this trip, and how she would put them to work once she was home again.

Shirley Parker, known to theater-goers as Dale Arden, looked forward to a new play. She felt thoroughly rested now, and the experiences she had had on the cruise would aid her immeasurably in interpreting future dramatic roles.

Lenora was thinking of the photographs she had taken during their voyage and what she would do with them when she got home. A number of the pictures had been taken for incorporation in feature stories which Beverly was to write about their trip, for the *Tribune*. Lenora owed the pictures first of all to the newspaper which employed her and Beverly, and which had reimbursed them very well for stories and pictures they had already sent to New York while on their journey. Still, there would be a number of pictures left which she might be able to work up into a book of her own. The idea pleased Lenora immensely.

Beverly thought of the wealth of information and experience she had absorbed during recent weeks, and of how she would use it in her writing career. In her trunk was the almost-completed manuscript of a new book. She had high hopes for it. She was full of new ambition and plans for the future. That is, she had been—until yesterday.

Yesterday, shortly after they dropped anchor in Honolulu, she had received a cablegram from her editor in New York. Halfway across the world had traveled the fateful words which put a dark shadow over her immediate future. No longer on the staff of the *Tribune?* Beverly could scarcely believe it. There had been no explanation, no reason given, only the words:

YOUR SERVICES NO LONGER REQUIRED.

Half-hoping that someone had made a mistake or was playing a bad joke, Beverly had wired Charlie Blaine asking for confirmation and an explanation. It wasn't like her editor to do such a thing and so heartlessly. He knew how much she loved her newspaper work. He had taught her patiently and kindly from the time she left college, until now she was an alert, capable member of his staff. Why should he then dismiss her so suddenly? She could think of nothing she had done which would merit such a dismissal. She had always been conscientious and sincere about her work. There *must* be some mistake!

"Don't worry, Bev!" Lenora gave her friend a quick hug. "Forget that silly old cable. Blaine couldn't do without us. There's been a stupid error somewhere." She stuck her head out of the porthole and took a deep breath.

"I'm glad we came back to Hawaii. Perhaps we can get in some more surfboard riding and swimming before we leave."

"It is the best place to take on the supplies we'll need for the long trip back across the Pacific," Shirley said, down on her knees searching for a missing shoe. "But if we're going to stop off in South America, I don't believe we can linger here very long."

A pounding on their cabin door interrupted her.

"Wake up, sleepyheads!" A masculine voice shouted. "The sun is shining, the trade winds are blowing, and breakfast is almost ready."

"The last interests me most at the moment," Lois said, rising with alacrity.

"Sleepyheads!" Lenora grunted. "I like that!

We haven't had more than five hours sleep. I shall take a long siesta this afternoon."

"You didn't have to sit up on deck until the wee hours," Lois teased her friend. "Just because there was a gorgeous moon, millions of stars, dance music on the radio—" Her voice faded in pleasant reminiscence.

"Go on," Lenora grinned. "You were up just as late as the rest of us."

"This station now signing off!" Lois giggled and disappeared into the bathroom.

Breakfast was a gay, informal affair, as were all their gatherings. As the group assembled, each member was in a different stage of wakefulness.

"It seems as though we had just gone to bed," Terry Cartwright grumbled with a yawn.

"Good morning, pet!" Lenora patted his arm consolingly. "Is ums still seepy? H-m-m?"

Terry bent a suspicious smile upon her. "You seem awfully bright and chipper this morning. Usually you're in a fog until noon."

"Not me," Lenora denied, turning her attention to the breakfast before her. "I'm wide awake the moment I open my eyes."

"That must be why you are putting sugar on your eggs," Lois remarked dryly.

The others laughed as Lenora put down the sugar with a cry of consternation.

Roger Garrett, their young skipper, was the only member of the group absent from the table. Halfway through the meal, he appeared with an envelope which he handed to Beverly.

"Evidently this is the answer to the cable you sent Blaine yesterday, Beverly," he said.

"Now we'll get this silly business straightened out!" Lenora exclaimed. "Open it, Bev."

Quickly Beverly tore open the envelope and read the brief message. For a moment she stared at the paper in her hand, then put the cable down and abruptly left the table. Larry rose immediately and followed her out.

Lenora retrieved the message from where Beverly had dropped it.

" 'NO MISTAKE,' " she read aloud. " 'YOUR CONNECTION WITH THIS PAPER IS HEREBY ENDED.' I can't believe it!" she exclaimed. "Poor Bev!" Then she, too, left the table to follow Beverly.

Lenora found Beverly and Larry at the stern rail. She went toward them slowly, wondering how she could best comfort her friend. She knew what pride Beverly took in her reporting and how much time and interest and effort she put into her work. This was a blow which would be hard to take.

"There are other newspapers, Bev," Lenora blurted out. "Don't feel too badly."

As Beverly turned to face the blonde girl, her dark eyes were stormy.

"I do feel badly," she said hotly, "but more than that, I'm—I'm mad! Charlie Blaine can't do this to me! He can't fire me without any reason or even one word of explanation, and I'm going to tell him so!"

"Hurrah for our side!" Lenora said in gleeful relief. "Bring your typewriter on deck and I'll stand by to fan the keys if they get too hot while you write your scorching—"

"I'm not going to write him," Beverly interrupted. "I'm going to fly back to New York and tell him personally!"

CHAPTER II

The Truth

"LET'S not be hasty about this," Lenora exclaimed. "Leave the *Susabella?* Fly all the way to New York—"

"To save my job, if I can," Beverly said firmly. "I want you all to go on with the cruise, and perhaps I will be able to rejoin you at another port."

"Larry, you talk to her," Lenora turned to Beverly's fiancé. "Don't let her break up our happy circle. The cruise won't be half as much fun without her. Unless—" Lenora's face brightened. "Unless I go with you?"

"No," Beverly said with a smile. "Stay with the cruise, Lenora, and if I can I will rejoin you. Honest, I will."

9

"Promise?"

Beverly nodded. "Now I must get busy. I'll only pack a few things. The *Susabella* can bring the rest home for me."

"If you're sure you really want to go, Bev, I'll see about your plane reservation," Larry offered.

"Will you?" Beverly asked eagerly. "Thanks, Larry. I'd like to leave on the first possible plane."

Larry departed immediately for the shore, and Beverly and Lenora went below to tell the others of Beverly's decision. As she had expected, there was a volley of protests, but Beverly could not be swayed. She was determined to discover why Charlie Blaine had dismissed her, and she felt that her protests would be more effective face to face. Her decision was finally accepted, and each of her friends set about doing what he could to speed her on her way.

Beverly had just come on deck when Larry returned from his trip ashore.

"I've got them!" Larry announced jubilantly, waving a long brown envelope above his head as he climbed on board. "Honolulu to San Francisco! The plane leaves in three hours. We haven't much time."

"We?" Beverly asked.

"I'm going with you, of course," Larry remarked with a smile.

That was why he hadn't tried to dissuade her, Beverly realized now.

"There is no reason for you to cut short your vacation," she began in protest and then smiled. "I suppose you've made up your mind."

"Whither thou goest—" Larry chuckled. "I don't like the idea of being separated from you for several weeks. Besides, darling, to tell the truth, I am a little tired of vacationing. I want to get back to work, too. There are big, new airplanes to be built and tested, and I aim to have a part in their design." He slipped his arm through hers. "Anyway, you might need someone to carry your bag."

The last few hours passed all too swiftly. It was hard to realize that while now Beverly and Larry idled in warm, glorious summer weather, soon they would step from a plane into a cool New York spring.

"It won't be the same on the *Susabella* without you," Shirley mourned as they waited at the airport until it was time for the travelers to board the giant airliner. "We are going to miss you two terribly."

"We'll miss you, too," Beverly replied soberly.

"You promised to rejoin us," Lenora reminded her anxiously.

"If I can," Beverly agreed.

"Send us a cable as soon as you land in New York," Lois added.

At that moment the signal came for all passengers to board the plane. There was a flurry of good-bye hugs and handshakes, and soon Beverly and Larry were in their places. The huge plane taxied down the runway and took to the air as gracefully and effortlessly as an eager bird.

"Homeward bound!" Beverly settled back into her seat with a sigh. "I can scarcely believe that it is all over. It was a wonderful vacation."

"Perhaps we can take another cruise sometime," Larry said, smiling. "There are lots of ports the *Susabella* hasn't visited yet."

Beverly said nothing. For some inexplicable reason, she felt she would never see the *Susabella* again. The feeling had first come to her as they left the yacht en route to the airport. She had looked back at the white bulk of the yacht riding easily on the gentle swell of water. Unbidden and uncalled for, the thought had occurred to her that she was seeing the ship for the last time. She wanted to feast her eyes on the trim, graceful lines of the craft, trying to remember each detail. There was absolutely no reason why such a premonition should come to her, and she attempted to dismiss it as part of her reluctance to part from her friends and miss the additional good times ahead of them. She assured herself that she would see the *Susabella* again when it dropped anchor in New York harbor.

Now, as Larry talked, the same swift, sad feeling came over her again. The *Susabella* was a thing of the past. Beverly would never see her again. Was it an omen? Was something going to happen to the boat—or to her?

Nine hours after taking off in Honolulu, the giant airplane deposited its passengers safely and without incident at San Francisco. From there, without wasting any time, another plane whisked Beverly and Larry through the night, across the continent to New York.

"Whenever I return to New York after a long trip I get the same thrill I felt the very first time I ever saw this town," Beverly declared, watching the city unfold in the early-morning mist.

"I know what you mean," Larry nodded. "It is all so familiar—and yet it seems new each time."

Tall buildings stretched up like fingers plucking at the clouds. Streets, like narrow ribbons, crawled with traffic. Boats, mere tiny toys adrift on slender threads of water, moved up the river. They were home, and soon they too would be swept up in the swift, fascinating pace of living. Home, after weeks of seeing strange sights, experiencing novel events, adventuring in far places. Home! It was a good feeling.

"I'll take you to your apartment first," Larry said presently. They had driven into New York City from LaGuardia Airport and had breakfasted together at Childs, after cabling the *Susabella* of their safe arrival. "Then I'll drop my bag at my place and go on out to see my boss—that is, unless you want me to come along and poke Blaine in the nose for you, Bev."

"That won't be necessary, Larry," Beverly replied, laughing. "I'll take care of Charlie Blaine myself. Call me later on," she added, "and I'll tell you what he said."

At the door of Mrs. Callahan's four-story, redbrick apartment house in the East Fifties, Beverly parted from Larry and ran up the stairs to the third floor. Everything in the apartment was just as they had left it. Their favorite chairs, books, pictures—all were in place and waiting for their owners.

Connie Elwood and Kathleen Ryan, former college friends of the girls, who occupied an apartment in the same building, had acted as custodians of their friends' possessions during their absence. There was a bond of staunch friendship between the six that nothing had ever broken.

Beverly paused only long enough to take a quick shower and change her clothes before she went upstairs to see Connie and Kathleen. Repeated tapping on her friends' door brought no response and her suspicions were confirmed. Both Kathleen and Connie already had left for their respective jobs. The reunion would have to wait until evening.

Beverly had left her car in Connie's charge during the cruise but had a duplicate ignition key in her desk drawer. After securing the key she picked up the car at the garage and then drove downtown. Within two blocks from the *Tribune* office, she found a place to park, then walked back to the *Tribune* building.

At the glass-paneled door she hesitated. Her hands were icy cold and her heart was racing. Her future depended upon what transpired within the next few minutes. In Honolulu she had been afire with righteous indignation over Blaine's treatment, but now that she was on his doorstep doubts and uncertainties began to crowd into her heart. She was as frightened now as she had been that first day, when she had come here looking for a job. In fact, Beverly thought, she was even more frightened now. If she really had been discharged from the paper, she must have failed in some way. If that was the case, it would be better to learn now what was wrong so that she could correct it. Perhaps Blaine would give her a second chance. Lifting her head, she pushed open the door and stepped inside.

The private world made up of people and material needed to keep alive a popular newspaper immediately surrounded her. She had long been an accepted member of the tribe, and she was greeted enthusiastically by everyone as she moved down the room between the rows of desks toward the glass-enclosed office where Charlie Blaine labored over his crowded desk.

Beverly's editor—shrewd brown eyes, hair beginning to turn gray, a round, pleasant face that gave no hint of the active, searching mind behind it—was speaking into the telephone when he saw Beverly pause at his door. Instantly he waved her in.

"Sit down, Bev, I'll be with you in a second." He motioned to a chair and continued with his telephone conversation. When he finished he smiled across his desk at her. "Hello! We didn't expect to see you in town for a long time yet."

"Is that why you sent me that cablegram?" Beverly asked without preliminary.

"Partly, yes," Blaine replied. He got to his feet and walked to the window. He talked with his back to her as he stared at the street below. "I'm sorry, Bev, but I had to give you that notice. We are cutting the staff and we won't need many feature writers."

"I've done some good news reporting for you, as well as feature stuff," Beverly reminded him. "I could hardly believe the wire when it came."

"I'm sorry if it spoiled your vacation," Blaine said tonelessly.

"I'm not thinking of my vacation," Beverly said bluntly. "I want to keep my job with the *Tribune*. Isn't there some way—"

Blaine shook his head. "I've thought it over carefully, Beverly. This is the only way."

Beverly felt stunned. There was not even the

possibility of a second chance. She was through here—through with the desk against the wall in the room outside, through with striving to make a deadline, through with the smell of printers' ink, through with racing about town to find news.

"I wouldn't believe the cablegram," Beverly said slowly. "I thought if I talked to you in person—"

"I didn't realize what a blow it would be to you," Blaine said with a worried frown. "Beverly, I—"

"If it is something I've done—" Beverly began.

Blaine crossed the room swiftly and put his arm about her shoulders.

"Don't think things like that, Bev. Go home and wait awhile—until things clear up. You'll have another job soon. There is a long writing career ahead of you."

"But not with the *Tribune*," Beverly said. "Well —thanks for everything."

She turned toward the door. She was angry and sick with disappointment. She was a good reporter—but not good enough for the *Tribune*. She saw all her hopes and plans going up in smoke.

"You can pick up the money for the last article

you sent me, at the cashier's window," Blaine called after her. "I'll see you soon, Bev."

"No, you won't!" Beverly retorted with a flash of spirit. "I never want to come into this office again!"

She banged the door to his office behind her so vigorously that Blaine caught his breath lest the glass shatter. Then he bent his head to hide a faint smile. Out of the corner of his eye he watched her progress past friendly co-workers to her own desk. He hated this part of his job, but this was the best way. When he finished reading the article before him, he stood up and reached for his hat.

Beverly, in turn, watched his progress through the office as she sat at her desk to remove the few articles in the drawers. She had always considered Blaine her good friend, but now he was treating her as if she were a stranger. Perhaps she had stayed away too long. She thought of how the girls had speculated in Hawaii. They had wondered if things at home were the same as when they had left. She could answer that now. Things were *not* the same.

"What's the matter, Bev?" A masculine voice cut into her thoughts and she looked up to see

Paul Thurmond, another reporter, approaching her desk. "Did you come home just to clean house?" He indicated the articles she was removing from the desk.

"I came home to be fired in person," she replied. "The *Tribune* henceforth can struggle along without my services."

"You're kidding!" Paul exclaimed.

"I wish I were," Beverly answered, and her voice shook a little, in spite of herself. "Do you know any place where an ex-reporter can get a job?"

"But Blaine always praised your work," Paul frowned. "We got a lot of complimentary letters on the stories you sent in from your cruise. He must be crazy, to let you go."

"I think so too," Beverly managed a grin, "but you always told me editors are crazy people."

"It is only their blue pencils that go crazy," Paul chuckled. "Seriously, Bev, what reason did he give?"

"Oh, cutting down the staff, not so much feature writing—" Beverly shrugged.

"Fairy tales!" Paul exclaimed. "He took on a new man last week."

"Then he must be intended for my job,"

Beverly said bitterly. "Well, I guess that is all." She picked up her things and looked about.

An unexpected lump rose in her throat and she knew she had better leave quickly, without any lingering farewells, if she didn't want the office force to see her in tears.

"See you, Paul."

"Sure," he said quickly, as if he understood. "Sure, Bev. I'll let you know if I hear of a job."

"Thanks," she flung over her shoulder and hastened toward the door.

Once outside, she stood undecided, breathing deeply of the cool air. It was almost time for lunch but she had no appetite. If she went home she might run into Kathleen, whose office was near by and who sometimes came home for lunch. Larry, too, might telephone or even come in person. She would have to make explanations about the loss of her job and she didn't feel up to doing it just yet. She must accustom herself to the idea that she was no longer a *Tribune* reporter. She didn't want her friends expressing shock and sympathy for her. When she told them about it she wanted at least to have a plan of action for the future. It would make it easier.

And Lenora! What would she tell Lenora? Her

friend would be waiting anxiously to hear what had happened. Lenora, she knew, would staunchly stand by her and refuse to continue working for the *Tribune* without her.

Beverly walked to where she had parked her car. A drive through the park might help to calm her. The traffic would not be so heavy there, and she would be able to do some thinking. She slid behind the wheel and the motor responded at once to her touch. As she released the brake, the door opposite her opened and a man slid onto the seat beside her.

"Drive away," he commanded. "Don't waste any time here."

CHAPTER III

The Plot

STARTLED, Beverly turned swiftly, and recognized the stocky figure.

"I no longer work for you, Mr. Blaine, and I do not have to take your orders now," she declared.

"You no longer work for the *Tribune*," Blaine corrected. "You do work for me. Come on, Beverly, get going!"

"What kind of a fairy tale is this?" Beverly demanded. "First I work for you, then I don't work for you, and now I do again—"

She swung the car into the traffic lane while she shook her head in bewilderment. "I think you'd better explain."

"You haven't had any lunch, have you?" Blaine asked. "Are you hungry?"

Beverly threw him a glance and saw a broad smile on his face. His eyes were twinkling and suddenly new hope was born in her. She began to feel better.

"Five minutes ago I couldn't have eaten anything, but now you may buy me a steak," she answered.

"Good! We'll drive out to Briggs' Cabin—steaks and chops de luxe. Go out across Washington Bridge," he suggested.

Beverly drove under his direction. It took them nearly an hour to reach their destination, and during that time Blaine made no conversation other than comments on the heavy traffic. Beverly decided that if he could wait, so could she, although she was bursting with curiosity. His remark, "You do work for me," had her puzzled—but happily so. Charlie Blaine had something up his sleeve and he would not reveal it until he was ready. For some reason he chose to be mysterious, getting into her car in that unexpected fashion, and now taking her to lunch a good distance away from the office. He had a reason and it would be a good one, of that she was sure.

Blaine directed her to park beside a sprawling log cabin just outside the glare of a red neon light.

He ushered her inside with great solicitude and gave the owner explicit directions about their steaks.

While he talked to the host, Beverly looked about her. They could enjoy comparative privacy in one of the high-backed booths that were built all around the room. The place was expensively modeled to look simple and rustic. She hoped the food would be as well prepared as appearances indicated.

"First of all," Blaine smiled at her, "let me say, thank goodness for your fighting spirit."

"Did you bring me here to fight with me?" Beverly asked, puzzled.

"I sent you a cablegram, and because of your fighting spirit you came six thousand miles to fight with *me*," he corrected. "I counted on your doing just that."

"I don't understand," Beverly frowned. "If this is all a big joke—"

"Believe me, it is no joke," Blaine assured her.

"Then what is it?" Beverly demanded. "Why did you want me to come all the way from Hawaii?"

"I wanted you back in town, but I didn't want anyone to know I sent for you."

"I'm here now," Beverly said. "You better explain."

"How well can you keep a secret?" Blaine asked. "And I do mean secret! No one is to know of your activities—absolutely no one—other than myself."

"You are being very mysterious," Beverly declared. "What is it all about?"

"It is about a job," Blaine replied. "I don't know where it will lead you or what you will find yourself involved in, but I want to learn the truth about a certain matter."

"You've got several excellent reporters in the office," Beverly said. "Why did you send six thousand miles for me?"

"I want someone I can trust implicitly and someone who I think can adapt herself to any circumstances. I've got other reporters, yes, but they *look* like reporters. Anyone would know what they were up to after a second glance. Also, I think a girl will be able to learn facts a man might not."

"You are certainly weaving an elaborate plot," Beverly declared. "I hope the subject is worth it."

"I'll tell you about it and you can judge for yourself," Blaine said.

He lowered his voice and glanced around before he began his story.

"Have you ever heard the name Barton? John K. Barton?"

"The millionaire?" Beverly asked. "Anyone who reads the newspapers knows the name. He is one of the richest men in America."

"And one of the unhappiest," Blaine agreed. "I know him quite well. He and I were friends long before he made his fortune, and our friendship has never changed. I want to help him and his son."

"What is their trouble?" Beverly wanted to know. "With all the money they have—"

"You missed the headlines recently," Blaine interrupted. "Young Philip Barton was taken into custody by agents of the Treasury Department under suspicion of smuggling counterfeit money into this country."

"If his father has so much money, why is Philip 'making' his own?" Beverly asked, smiling.

"He isn't," Blaine said shortly. "At least, I hope not. Philip has always been a weak character, but he isn't really a bad boy. From the time he was small he has been cursed with too much money. Everything he wanted his father bought him.

Whenever Phil got into trouble his father and his money were there to pull him out of it. In college he cared nothing for studies or campus activities. His chief interest was in enjoying himself—until he was dismissed. That nearly broke his father's heart, because he had wanted Philip to study law and make something of himself. I think that was when John Barton began to realize that he had thoroughly spoiled his son. In order to rectify the mistake he had made, he became stern with Philip, cut off his allowance, practically drove him out of the house to stand on his own feet. His harshness is like a stone wall between them.

"A few months ago I convinced John that he should make one last gesture for Philip, so he bought the boy a freight airline in Florida. It was a new business, but since Philip has always loved airplanes his father and I thought it might be his salvation. It would give him a dominating interest and something to work for. It is John Barton's last attempt to make a man of his son. He has warned Philip that if he fails with this enterprise, as he has with everything else, he will be disinherited and need never expect help from his father again."

"That should make Philip sit up and take notice," Beverly commented dryly.

"You would think so," Blaine nodded. "Philip isn't a bad boy at heart. He is really quite likable, but he is weak, and any rosy picture can lure him away from his duty and obscure his better judgment."

"What has this to do with me?" Beverly wanted to know. "I certainly don't want to be governess to a spoiled young man like that."

Blaine smiled. "Wait, there is more to the story. Philip took charge of the airline and seemed to be making progress. He began to have a series of minor misfortunes, but he was bent on making a success of the enterprise. I visited him once and he took a genuine pride in showing me around. Then one of his planes crashed on the way back from a flight to South America. In the wreckage the authorities found a package of counterfeit money. Neither the pilot of the plane, a man named Lennet, nor Philip could account for its being there. Both Philip and Lennet were taken into custody by the T-men but later were released for lack of conclusive evidence. However, the affair received a lot of publicity and was the final blow for John Barton. Philip feels that he was hounded and exploited by the newspapers. He has threatened to have all reporters run off the field if they come near him again, even friends of his. That's the reason I wanted everyone to know you had been discharged. Philip knows Paul Thurmond and several of the other boys, and if the question should ever come up, they could honestly tell Philip that you're no longer a reporter. Otherwise, you'd never even get to first base."

"And does Mr. Barton really think Philip is a counterfeiter?" Beverly inquired.

"He is afraid he might be, but I still can't believe the boy would have anything to do with the smuggling of fake money."

"Are you sure?" Beverly asked shrewdly.

"It is mostly wishful thinking," Blaine admitted. "I like Philip and I want to make sure. I have had a tip that the Treasury agents still suspect that counterfeit money is coming into Miami. From there, they think, the money is being shipped west for distribution. They have been unable to definitely tie the shipments to the Barton Airline, but Philip will not be free of suspicion until the real culprits are caught."

"You still haven't told me where I enter the story," Beverly said.

"I want you to go to Miami, get a job with the

Barton Airline, and keep your eyes and ears open. See what you can learn. Find out if counterfeit money is coming in on Barton planes and find out if Philip himself is involved. You will not be acting as a reporter, Bev. You will be acting as my agent."

"Why don't you hire a private investigator?" Beverly asked. "He could get the truth better than I."

"Any more publicity like the last and John Barton will refuse to see his son again ever," Blaine said. "I am a newspaperman, but this is one time I don't want any publicity, Bev. I am counting on you to see that no discovery you may make gets into the news—unless it will clear Philip. If it doesn't clear Philip—" Blaine sighed. "Well, then it will be my job to see that the T-men get Philip's full cooperation. You are to work solely as a private agent," Charlie went on, "and report to me by telephone at my home. I want to impress upon you that this job is strictly for me personally, and no one is to know what you are doing."

"Maybe Philip won't give me a job," Beverly said. "Is his business booming? Will he need any additional help?"

"No, his business isn't booming," Blaine said. "I don't care how you manage it, but I want you to establish yourself with the Barton Airline and get the truth of the matter for me. I want you to find the real counterfeiters if you can. That means we must observe the utmost secrecy—for your own protection—secrecy here as well as in Miami."

"It sounds like a large order." Beverly frowned. "The Treasury agents haven't got at the truth yet, but I am supposed to. I should have studied to be a magician instead of a newspaperwoman."

Blaine grinned. "I count on your resourcefulness. You've gotten a lot of good stories for the *Tribune* in the time you've been with us. If I didn't think you could do this for me I would never have assigned it to you. Secrecy means a good deal because of the Barton name. All the papers put it in headlines on the faintest excuse. If Philip gets into any more scrapes and lands in the headlines again, I am afraid he and his father will never be reconciled. It means a great deal to me to learn the truth. If you are successful, Bev, it will mean a raise in salary. And, of course, your old job on the paper will be waiting when you get back."

"The things I do for the dear old *Tribune*," Beverly smiled. "When do I start?"

"As soon as you can," Blaine responded promptly. "I'll give you a check now that will cover your expenses for the next couple of weeks, until you know where you're going to be. And remember, Bev, it is a secret—yours and mine."

CHAPTER IV

The Deception Begins

THE ride back to the city was accomplished in
haste so that Blaine could get back to his desk.

After she dropped Blaine a block from the
Tribune office, Beverly drove to the girls' apartment. Without bothering to turn on the lights, she
crossed the room and flung the window wide to the
spring night air. Dusk was stealing over New
York. Lights were beginning to glow in the win-
dows. Somewhere a clock chimed. A radio was
blaring out late news bulletins, and a chorus of
automobile horns rose on the air. Beverly leaned
on the window sill and contemplated the city. It
was a mass of tall buildings, rumbling traffic, busy
workers, idlers—many people with many dreams.

There was the sound of a door opening behind her, and Beverly turned quickly about. A girl was silhouetted against the light from the hall.

"Eek!" Connie Elwood let out a muffled cry.

"Come in, Connie!" Laughing, Beverly switched on a lamp.

Connie dropped onto the couch and let out a deep sigh.

"You scared the wits out of me, Beverly! I thought I was seeing a ghost. What are you doing here? Are the other girls with you? Why didn't you let us know you were coming home?"

Beverly quickly explained to her sandy-haired friend the reason for her presence in the city while the others continued their vacation.

"You mean Charlie Blaine actually discharged you?" Connie gasped. "I can't believe it!"

"I couldn't believe it either," Beverly replied. "That is why I flew home."

"Your work for the paper has always been so good," Connie protested. "We loved the stories you sent in from your cruise. Why would Blaine do such a thing? Did he give you a good reason?"

Beverly was about to make a cautious reply, when the sound of running footsteps was heard in the hall and the door burst open. Vivacious, plump, rosy-cheeked Kathleen Ryan whirled in.

"Is Bev here? I saw the light from the street and thought something was wrong until I saw her car parked at the curb. Where did you descend from, chum?" She hugged Beverly.

"Descend is right." Connie laughed. "She and Larry flew home from Hawaii."

"Why? What brought you back from the far corners of the world?" Kathleen wanted to know. "Did you run out of places to visit?"

"Far from it," Beverly replied, laughing. "The world is too big not to offer something new for each day."

"Bev has lost her job on the paper," Connie told her friend, with a frown. "Did you ever hear of such a thing?"

"You don't really mean that!" Kathleen exclaimed.

"It is the truth!" Connie insisted. "She was just telling me about it when you came in."

Beverly repeated her story for Kathleen's benefit, trying to put the right shade of feeling into her words. Her friends must believe that she was through with the paper. They must believe that she was discouraged and disappointed. This was the beginning of the deception Charlie Blaine had warned her about. Why she returned to New York could be the truth, but from now on she must keep her secret and weave a story to rival the fiction which emerged from her typewriter. From this day until the case of the counterfeiters was closed, she must live two lives—one of the normal Beverly Gray which her friends could share, and the other of spy and investigator about which only Blaine could know.

Beverly was glad that Lenora was thousands of miles away. Her blonde friend was too sharp and knew Beverly's passion for newspaper work too well to believe that she would forsake the battle to hold her job as reporter. Connie and Kathleen knew her love for the job she had held, too, but apparently they believed the story she told them.

"Wait until Katharine Merrill hears about this!" Connie exclaimed. "You two were such rivals, I bet she will be relieved that you aren't a reporter now."

"We were friendly rivals," Beverly said, smiling.

Katharine Merrill was a reporter for a rival newspaper, and though the two girls were often in keen competition for exclusive news, they were also friends. Now, however, Beverly was glad that Charlie Blaine had kept this assignment such a secret. She knew Kay would be eager to get a big story about John K. Barton and his son—as would every other paper. If there was the faintest suggestion that Beverly was on a secret assignment, Kay would not rest until she had discovered what it was. And Charlie Blaine would never forgive Beverly if anything like that happened.

"Maybe Kay could get you a job on her paper," Connie suggested.

"No, thanks!" Beverly returned quickly.

"What do you plan to do?"

"Oh—" Beverly was evasive. "I'll find some kind of a job."

"We need another girl in the office," Kathleen said eagerly. "I could speak to Mr. Gerard about you."

"No, thanks," Beverly said hastily.

It hadn't occurred to her that she might run into difficulty this way. Her well-meaning friends would, of course, want to help her find another position.

"I think I will go visit some friends out of town for a while," she explained. "When I return I'll look for another job, but not yet."

"If we can do anything at all to help," Kathleen assured her, "you have only to let us know."

The telephone rang insistently at that point. It was Larry with plans for the evening.

"I've been fortunate enough to get tickets for the new musical 'Spring is Late,' " he said. "After dinner and the show, we'll dance and get reacquainted with our town. What do you say?"

"It sounds like a lot of fun," Beverly exclaimed.

"Good! I'll see you in about an hour. Bev— what did Blaine say? Did he really fire you?"

Beverly hesitated. Blaine had said that positively no one was to know the truth. She hated to be evasive with Larry, but she had promised her editor.

"Yes, he did," she answered slowly.

Larry was silent for a moment.

"Don't feel too badly, Bev. We'll talk about it tonight. Maybe I know a solution for your future."

Larry was determinedly cheerful when he called for Beverly. The musical comedy which they attended was bright and gay. Afterward, they went to the Starlight Roof to dance. The magic and color of New York surrounded them the entire evening.

"Our adopted town," Beverly sighed as they paused to look at the lights of the city spread out below. "I love it. I love the noise and the crowds and the bright lights."

"A week ago you were just as happy on a little island in the Pacific," Larry said, smiling.

"I love the lions at the library, they look so majestic," Beverly continued dreamily. "I like to ride the Staten Island ferry, and feed the squirrels in Central Park. I like the big shopwindows showing the latest styles, and the roller coaster at Coney Island. And did you ever see the sun come up over the—"

"Our crowd has seen the sun come up in lots of strange places," Larry reminded her, chuckling.

"But New York's my home," Beverly said. "I guess that is why it seems best. Funny, isn't it?"

"That isn't funny, but I think something else is," Larry commented dryly. "I think there is something amiss with *my* miss."

"Whatever do you think it is, Doctor Owens?" Beverly asked with a teasing glance.

"Either you are an excellent actress—"

"Shirley is the actress," Beverly replied.

"Something is wrong," Larry insisted. "Of course I'm glad to see you as happy as you seem to be tonight, but it puzzles me. It isn't what I expected. You loved your job with the *Tribune*. You didn't give it up without a struggle. Your cheerfulness and the loss of your job don't go together."

"I am not the tearful type," Beverly said, looking away from him. "Did you expect me to spend the evening sobbing on your shoulder?"

"I only want to know what it is you are keeping from me," Larry said firmly.

Beverly slipped her arm within his.

"I did not lie about my job. I am not working for the *Tribune* any more. Let's go in and dance and think about something more pleasant for the rest of the evening."

"If you aren't working for the *Tribune*, why not marry me? If you have no job to worry about, why don't you worry about me?" He grinned. "What do you say, Bev? Shall we have a spring wedding?"

"I'll be happy to throw rice at the bride," a gay voice interrupted. "Sorry, but we couldn't help overhearing."

Beverly and Larry turned to see Kay Merrill and her escort.

"Then it is true, Bev, about you leaving the ranks of the newshounds," Kay said after the first greetings were over. "I won't say I'm sorry. You took too many headlines away from me."

"The headlines are all yours now," Beverly

said. "I am leaving for Florida soon, and I haven't decided what I will do when I return."

She hadn't told Larry yet about Florida, and while the four of them talked she watched his face for a sign of his reaction to the news. When Kay and her friend left them Beverly and Larry went inside to dance.

"Is Florida more important than our future together?" he asked, as his arm went about her waist.

"It isn't that, Larry," Beverly protested. "It is just that I—"

"When will you return? Next month? What are you going to Florida for? I thought you loved New York!" There was bitterness in his tone.

"Don't be angry, Larry," Beverly pleaded. "I'm going to do something for a friend—"

"Blaine!" Larry exclaimed. "That cable from Blaine started all this. What fancy little plot has he woven this time? Why all the secrecy? Shall I go to Florida with you? We could make it our honeymoon!"

"I can't marry you right now, Larry. Trust me for a little while longer," Beverly said earnestly. "It is true, I am going to Florida for Blaine, but I can't explain about it and no one must know.

Larry, we promised each other a few weeks ago that we wouldn't have any more misunderstandings, remember?"

"I don't want to quarrel with you, Bev, but when we are apart I imagine all sorts of things happening to you. Suppose you need help down in Florida?"

"Then I will send for you," she said impulsively, never dreaming that the words would come true.

"That's a promise!" Larry said quickly. "If anything comes up that you can't handle, you will send for me and I'll fly down in my plane."

"I promise," Beverly agreed lightly, "and now let's dance!"

CHAPTER V

A New Job

AT FIRST Beverly thought she would fly to Miami, but later she decided that she might want to use her car while she was there, so she drove all the way. She followed the main highways and stayed overnight in the cities. It gave her plenty of time to think about Charlie Blaine's assignment and to plan her campaign.

Once in Miami, she checked in at a downtown hotel and set about learning what she could about the Barton Airline. The company advertised in the newspapers: "We'll fly your freight at a reasonable rate," and there was a small map showing the route of the line.

It was a bright, sunny morning when Beverly started out to drive the distance from Miami to the Barton Airline office and airfield. The highway was smooth and straight, with thick green foliage bordering the road. About halfway to her destination she came upon an automobile stalled in the middle of the road. A young man, about Larry's age, was pushing it and perspiring freely in the hot sun. Beverly felt sorry for him and slowed down.

As she drew closer she saw that he was about six feet tall, with blond hair and a deep tan. He had a pleasant if not particularly impressive manner. He waved her to a halt and asked for help.

"Would you mind pushing my car to the service station about half a mile down the road?"

Beverly agreed and he hopped into his car. Slowly the two vehicles proceeded along the highway, Beverly's car providing the momentum. They turned off the road at the service station, and the young man came back to thank Beverly.

"You certainly were an answer to my prayers that time," he declared. "Once the attendant puts a new battery in my car, I can be on my way. Thanks a lot!"

The young man watched and waved after her as Beverly took to the highway again. The rest of the drive to the airfield was without incident. She parked in the small parking lot and got out of the car to watch two men loading an assortment of crates and boxes into a plane on the runway. No one paid any attention to her.

Beside the parking lot was a low, one-story, white stucco building. From a flagpole atop the building dangled a worn gray windsock scarcely moving in the breeze.

Beyond the white building were two large hangars, both sadly in need of paint. The whole appearance of the place was one of neglect.

Beverly had been standing there about a half-hour, watching the loading of the plane and wondering how she should go about getting a job, when another car drew up beside hers and the young man she had helped on the highway got out.

"Hi," he said in surprise. "What are you doing in this neighborhood?"

"Trying to get up the courage to go inside and ask for a job," Beverly said. "Do you work here?"

His face twisted in a wry grin.

"Yes, I work here. They aren't looking for any new help. What made you come here? Not a reporter, are you?"

Wary of the questioning look he gave her, Beverly shrugged her shoulders and assumed a nonchalance she was far from feeling.

"No. I just like airplanes. I saw the Barton Airline ad in the newspaper and thought perhaps I could find a spot in the office."

"It is too bad," he frowned. "I'd like to help you. What can you do?"

"Typing, filing—I have a private pilot's license," Beverly added hopefully.

"I hate to discourage you, but I don't think the Barton Airline can afford another employee right now." He sighed.

"What's the trouble?" Beverly inquired.

"You must have read about it in the papers," he returned. "Everyone did."

"You mean about finding counterfeit money on that plane that crashed? That was unfortunate," Beverly agreed, "but I believe I will talk to Mr. Barton anyway."

"You are talking to Mr. Barton," he told her, grinning.

"You?" Beverly was genuinely surprised. He was not a bit as she had expected him to be. She was glad she hadn't said anything more.

"I'm afraid there wouldn't be much of a future

for you here," he said. "If I were you, I'd go back to town and get a job somewhere else."

"But I like airplanes and I'm not afraid of hard work," Beverly persisted. She looked about at the buildings. "I'll admit it does look rather run-down, but maybe there is something I can do to help. I'd like to try," Beverly pleaded. "I won't expect much salary at first. There must be some office work I can do."

"Such persistence!" He smiled. "Very well, come along, but don't say I didn't warn you! You're hired for as long as the company lasts—or as long as you want to stay."

They walked together to the office, and young Barton pushed open one of the heavy glass doors to the building.

There was a girl at the switchboard, which served as a reception desk also, and beyond her was a hall from which opened two more doors. At the end of the hall was a third door giving access to the flying field.

"Thelma, this is Miss—" Barton paused and glanced at the girl by his side. "My good Samaritan," he finished. "You *do* have a name, don't you?"

Beverly supplied it, and the blonde girl responded with a bright smile and nod of the head.

"Miss Gray is going to work with us," Barton said. "Show her around, Thelma. Walter can assign her duties. I'll see you later," he told Beverly and went down the hall through the door to the field.

"I didn't know he was going to take on any more help," Thelma Chase said, leaving her desk to join Beverly.

"He didn't know it himself," Beverly replied, smiling. "I persuaded him to give me a job."

"There are a lot of reports to be typed," Thelma continued, leading the way down the hall to a large room where three desks were littered with papers and the drawers to a filing cabinet stood untidily ajar.

"I hate office work myself," Thelma confided. "I'm glad you are here."

A thin, red-haired individual turned from the table at which he had been working and came toward them.

"This is Walter Baker," Thelma explained. "He does the bookkeeping and manages the office."

From the first introduction, Beverly neither trusted nor liked her new co-worker. His cold green eyes and narrow, pointed chin made her think of a fox. The way he studied her and his soft-spoken questions were irritating.

Thelma went back to the desk and switchboard in the hall, and Walter Baker led Beverly to a desk by the window.

"I'll be glad to help you all I can," he told her. "I believe you will find everything you need right now in the desk drawers. There is plenty of work to do, though I don't know how he is going to pay your salary. You might begin by typing these reports in duplicate. Thelma and I will be going out to lunch in an hour. Will you join us?"

Beverly agreed, and when he moved away she sat down at the untidy desk. It was obvious that efficiency was not the keynote of the place. How could any business prosper with such dilatory employees?

A plane's motors broke into a deafening roar and Beverly looked up. From her desk she had a clear view of the runway and she could watch the silver plane from the time it taxied into position on the runway until it was airborne.

"At least I like the view," she commented to herself, as she began to sort the array of papers before her.

The hour until lunchtime flew past, and Thelma and Walter called her. In Thelma's car they drove a half-mile down the road to a small eating place for a light lunch.

Thelma chattered a great deal on various subjects, but Walter said little at first. When he did speak it was generally to ask Beverly a question about herself. She, in turn, tried to learn what she could about the business.

"Whatever made you want to work at the Barton Airline?" Thelma asked, giggling. "I should think you would want a job in town. There's nothing to do out here in this lonely spot except go fishing."

"Ugh! Awful thought!" exclaimed Walter Baker.

"I like airplanes," Beverly returned with a smile.

"Perhaps she has designs on Mr. Barton," Walter suggested jokingly. "A job for love—that sort of thing. He isn't married, but I believe that he is interested in some girl in Miami."

"I never met Mr. Barton until this morning," Beverly assured them with a smile.

"We'll have to guess again, Walter," Thelma laughed. "Perhaps Miss Gray is a New York reporter playing spy and looking for a story for her newspaper—not that the airline hasn't been in enough headlines already."

With a start Beverly realized that she had been thinking of Thelma as a lighthearted, frivolous individual who probably did no more than necessary to earn her salary. Now she suddenly realized that there was a quick, shrewd mind behind Thelma's giddiness. Already she must have spotted the New York license plates on Beverly's car. It might very well be Thelma who would guess Beverly's secret if she were not constantly on her guard.

"How many pilots does Mr. Barton have working for him?" Beverly asked, to change the subject.

"Only one," Thelma answered. "He had three, but he had to let the other two go when he couldn't get enough business to keep them busy."

"Why can't he get more business?" Beverly asked. "Wasn't the line well established when he took it over?"

"It was prosperous enough," Walter commented with a shrug. "Someone else could make a big success of it. Barton lost a lot of business because he didn't make shipments on time."

"Why couldn't he meet his schedules?" Beverly persisted.

"Something always seemed to be happening to one or another of the planes to ground it," Thelma answered. "Orders got mixed up, cargo was damaged—" She broke off. "My, you *are* curious, aren't you?"

"I like to know about the business I am working for," Beverly answered. "Of course, I read the newspaper story about the trouble Mr. Barton and his pilot were in over that counterfeit money. What's your opinion about all that?"

"I haven't any," Thelma answered. "It is all a mystery to me."

"And me," Walter agreed. "But I don't think Barton has the brains to do anything like that. All his life he has been Papa's Boy, and now that he is on his own he is lost."

"It sounds as if you don't think much of your boss," Beverly said dryly.

"I do everything he requires of me, but if I didn't do more than that, we'd be out of business already," Walter retorted. "Shall we go back to the office?"

"Was that a Barton plane I saw take off this morning?" Beverly asked as they rose to go.

"No, that belonged to another line. It merely stopped to pick up some freight that should have gone out yesterday."

"Where is the Barton plane?"

"En route from South America," Thelma answered.

"How often is a flight scheduled to South America?" Beverly inquired.

"Whenever there is a shipment to be made," Thelma replied with a shrug. "They used to be a regular event, but lately—"

"There won't be many more," Walter prophesied. "Barton might as well give up right now."

CHAPTER VI

Air Pirates

THE more involved Beverly became in the duties she had to perform, the more shocked she was at the haphazard manner in which the company was run. In her opinion, Philip Barton trusted Walter Baker and Thelma Chase far too much. Those two needed close supervision to make sure that their work was done completely and accurately. As it was, Philip entered the office only once during that first day and then only to hand Beverly an invoice and ask her to type it for him. Couldn't he see how wrong things were here? Didn't he know what to expect from competent help? He seemed content to spend most of his time helping his one remaining mechanic work on the airplanes. Beverly could see them now through the window beside her desk. Didn't Philip realize that the success of his business could be made or ruined here in the office as well as in the hangars? Obviously he was not the businessman his father was.

When Beverly saw young Barton coming toward the office building she picked up the typed invoice and took it to the small room across the hall, which served as his private office. Philip looked worried and kept glancing from his watch to the window.

"Is anything wrong?" Beverly asked while she waited for him to initial the bill.

"Our flight from San Joanna was due at two o'clock," he replied. "It is three now."

As he finished speaking, the telephone rang and Philip leaped to answer it.

"Yes! Lennet!" There was a mixture of relief and anxiety in his voice. "Where are you? What's happened?"

Beverly lingered by the door, openly listening to Philip's end of the conversation. It was obvious that the two o'clock plane was in difficulties. This was the stuff of which headlines were made. She wanted to learn what she could, even though she would not be the reporter to write about it.

"Stolen?" Philip shouted into the telephone. "How? Where are you?"

The pilot unfolded a curious tale, and later, when Philip repeated it to her, Beverly could scarcely believe it.

"Lennet says he was only about fifty miles from here when someone—a stowaway—attacked him in the air, knocked him unconscious, and landed him in a lonely field. Then the unknown assailant made off with the plane and cargo."

"Pirates in the air?" Beverly was skeptical. "How did the unknown person get aboard the plane?"

"Probably stowed away when the cargo was being loaded," Philip replied. He paced nervously up and down the office. "This is a fine mess. I'm left with only two planes and I will need at least three to take care of my contracts—if I get the new one I'm after. I'm going to call the police!"

"Where is the pilot now?" Beverly asked.

"On his way here. We may learn more when he arrives," Barton said. "You certainly didn't join a lucky outfit, Miss Gray."

"Were the plane and cargo insured?" Beverly asked.

"Yes." Philip shook his head. "I don't understand. Stealing an airplane—"

"It is hard to believe," Beverly agreed. "Has the pilot been in your employ a long time?"

"Ever since I took over the line," Philip said. "I've always trusted him."

"Has he ever had trouble before?" Beverly asked.

Barton looked at her quietly for a moment.

"He was piloting the plane on which they found the counterfeit money," he said slowly. "But I am sure Lennet was innocent. If he were only after money and profit he would have left me long ago. He could command a higher salary on any other airline than what I am paying him. I think he stays with me for friendship's sake."

"I see," Beverly nodded slowly.

"I don't know why I am telling you all this, Miss Gray," Philip Barton smiled, "except that somehow I feel I can trust you."

Beverly felt herself blushing. In her capacity as private investigator she was plotting to betray his confidence to Charlie Blaine. Beverly Gray, the Mata Hari of Miami, she thought. In the end, however, she might be able to help rather than trick him.

Philip picked up the phone to report to the police about the unusual robbery, and Beverly went back to her own desk. She found it hard to concentrate upon her work. Over and over she kept wondering why Barton's plane had been stolen. Of course, Philip Barton, with his lack of business sense, was a good target for any scheming individual. Philip might have been reckless and incorrigible in college, but when it came to running a business he was as innocent as a child. When John K. Barton bought the airline for his son, she thought, he should have given him lessons in how to handle the business.

About an hour later the pilot, Lennet, arrived, making a grand entrance with much noise and excitement. The bold, dashing, adventurous type, he included Beverly in his general salutation to the office.

"Behold, the eagle that walked home!"

Then, laughing uproariously at his own witticism, he went on his way to Philip's private office. Big and brash and full of vitality, he was nevertheless a likable person. But Beverly still saw him through a cloud of suspicion. After all, it *was* on his wrecked plane that the counterfeit money had been found, and he had just lost another of his company's planes—a loss which might easily cripple his employer's chance to land the new contract he was after.

Beverly wondered just how bad the company's financial position was. Perhaps Barton was not so dejected over the loss of the plane as he pretended to be. The insurance money he would receive for the plane and cargo might provide a nice sum of working capital. Had he instructed his pilot to "lose" the plane in order to collect the insurance money?

Lennet stuck his head in the door and called Walter Baker.

"Hey, Walt! Come on into the boss's office for a conference."

Beverly watched the bookkeeper leave the room. She was alone in the office, and on Walter's desk were the company ledgers. Now was her chance. The figures entered there should tell her whether the company was operating at anything like a profit or whether the position was such that Barton would take desperate measures to better it.

Quickly Beverly slipped across the room. She sat down at Walter's desk and opened the ledger. At first she could barely understand his writing, but as she studied the columns of figures before her it became increasingly clear that the Barton

Airline was on the verge of bankruptcy. Once more Philip Barton would be a failure in his father's eyes. This time it would cost him not only the airline but also his inheritance. Charlie Blaine had told her that Barton Senior would be through with Philip if he did not make a go of this enterprise. Philip would have nothing left if he lost his freight airline. His whole future depended upon his keeping his business together.

"Do you find that interesting reading, Miss Gray?"

Walter Baker's voice was heavy with fury as he came up behind Beverly.

For a moment she felt frozen to the chair. She had not expected to be caught in the act of snooping. Baker had entered so noiselessly that she had not had any warning.

"Yes," she said, striving to appear calm and cool. "I find the books very interesting. In fact, it looks as though I may not have a job much longer."

"I suggest you do not wait for the end of the Barton Airline but find another place to do your spying."

"What do you mean?" Beverly asked coldly.

"You ask too many questions, Miss Gray," Walter declared. "Your duties are typing and filing—not snooping in the ledgers or worrying about things that do not concern you."

"Since I am working here, the future of the Barton Airline does concern me," Beverly retorted. "I would like to help Mr. Barton make a success of his business. I am sure he hopes all his employees feel the same way."

For a moment Walter studied her in silence.

"I can find a way to make you leave," he said slowly. "For one thing, Mr. Barton thoroughly dislikes reporters and newspapers. In the past few weeks they have caused him a lot of headaches and helped to alienate him from his father. If I told him I have reason to believe that you are a reporter and are here solely to gather information for more unfavorable publicity about him, he would discharge you immediately."

"I don't believe it," Beverly said, quelling the panic in her heart. "He trusts me."

"He wouldn't—in the face of what I would tell him," Walter assured her bitterly. "I shall tell him you are a reporter sent here to spy upon him, unless—"

"Unless what?" Beverly wanted to know.

"Unless you leave the Barton Airline at once and never return!"

CHAPTER VII

Suspicions

"I DON'T intend to leave," Beverly said flatly. "I did not know you considered the ledgers a secret. Why shouldn't I be interested in seeing how sound the company is? If the Barton Airline goes bankrupt I shall be out of work again."

"Why didn't you ask me about the financial status of the company?" Walter shot at her.

"It didn't occur to me to wonder about it until I realized how upset Mr. Barton is over the loss of the plane. You were in his office, the books were here—" Beverly shrugged.

"And do you intend to use the knowledge you now have about the company?" Walter demanded. "I suppose you will immediately publicize it."

"I shall not tell anyone," Beverly replied quietly.

"I do not believe you are telling me the truth," Walter said, "but we shall see."

Beverly went back to her desk and resumed her work. Baker had told her frankly that he did not believe her story, but evidently he did not intend to take any immediate action in the matter. Beverly half expected him to go to Philip Barton at once, but as time passed and he did not leave his desk she began to breathe easier.

Her suspicions of Walter began to grow. Barton evidently trusted his bookkeeper implicitly. But if Walter was keeping honest books, why should he be so upset when someone looked at them? What had he been afraid she would learn from them?

"What on earth were you and Walter fussing about?" Thelma asked when Beverly brought the outgoing mail to her desk. "I peeked in once, but I thought I'd better not interrupt."

"He was angry because I looked at his precious ledgers," Beverly replied. "He is a suspicious soul, isn't he?"

"Walter is always thinking of the company and what might happen to it," Thelma commented.

"It is almost five o'clock," she added. "Why don't you go home?"

"I have something to finish," Beverly replied.

"Oh, go on home," Thelma urged. "There is no hurry about the work. It will wait until to-morrow morning."

"Will you ride into town with me?" Beverly invited, hoping she would have a chance to talk to the girl privately and perhaps learn more about Philip Barton and Walter Baker.

"Thanks, but I have to work late," Thelma answered. "I'm stuck with the insurance reports about the lost plane, and besides, Mr. Barton is afraid the newspapermen will come out here ask-ing questions, and he wants me to keep them away from him. You go on. By the way, where do you live in Miami?"

"At the Chalfont Hotel," Beverly answered. "I haven't anything special to do this evening. I'll work in your place if you want to go home," she offered.

"No indeed!" Thelma exclaimed. "Thanks just the same. You run along. I'll see you to-morrow."

"I might as well stay, too," Beverly said. "We can go home together when you have finished."

"No," Thelma said rather sharply. An impatient frown crossed her face. "I am sure Mr. Barton wouldn't want you to think he is a hard taskmaster by having to work overtime your very first day."

Thelma's whole attitude began to strike Beverly as odd. It certainly seemed as if the girl were trying to be rid of her.

"Careful!" Beverly told herself. "Don't overdo it or she will become suspicious."

"Very well," she said aloud. "I'll close up my desk. Good night, Thelma."

When Beverly left the building she went out through the door which opened onto the flying field. Lennet, the pilot, and Philip were standing at the entrance to No. 1 hangar, beside a huge silver plane which was to take off in the morning. This plane, and a smaller one in the second hangar, were now all that was left of the Barton Airline. The one which had been stolen was a duplicate of this one, and looking at it now, Beverly wondered how anyone could steal such a big craft and hope to conceal it.

The men saw her and walked over.

"Any word about the missing plane?" Beverly asked.

"None," Barton said with a heavy sigh. "The authorities are broadcasting an alarm, but so far they have sent me no news."

"How could anyone hide such a big thing?" Beverly wondered again, aloud.

"They may have headed out to sea and crashed it," Barton said, frowning.

"Why should anyone want to do that?" Beverly inquired.

Barton shrugged. "Someone might like to eliminate my competition for freight business," he said. "Allied Farms spend a big sum every year on air freight. I've been after their contract for a long time and I think it's just about in the bag. But others are after it, too. If I get it I must live up to every word of the contract, but now with only two planes—" He shook his head doubtfully.

"You couldn't buy another plane?" Lennet suggested.

"What would I use for money?" Barton asked. "Walter tells me our new financial statement will be even worse than the last."

"How about your father?" Lennet persisted. "Would he advance—"

"No, he wouldn't!" Philip exploded. "After the

mess we got into about the counterfeit money, he is just waiting for news that I'm in more trouble. He bought me this freight line just to get me away from New York and out of his sight."

"He might have had a good motive," Beverly said. "Perhaps he thought a business of your own—"

"Ha!" Philip scoffed. "You don't know my father! I've always been a nuisance to him."

"I don't believe that," Beverly returned. "I believe he only wants to be proud of you."

"Do you know my father?" Philip asked suspiciously.

"I've never met him," Beverly answered truthfully. "I've read about him in the newspapers."

"John K. Barton, financier and philanthropist," Philip murmured, kicking an unoffending pebble out of his path. "Kind and generous with everyone except his own son."

"It seems to me that he was generous enough if he bought you all this," Beverly commented, indicating the scope of the field.

"And I think he would be generous enough again to buy you another plane," Lennet commented. "You can appeal to his business sense. With another plane you could fulfill your contracts. It would be a good investment for him."

"I won't appeal to my father for anything," Philip said stubbornly. "He told me he was through financing me. He bought me the business and tossed me into it to sink or swim."

"Phil, I have a little money—" Lennet began.

"No," Barton interrupted. "Walter has offered to help, too. He's even willing to raise some money and buy me out. But I'm not going to borrow from my friends. I'll save the line somehow. I've got to!" he said earnestly.

"We will all do our best to help you," Beverly said at once.

"I'm sorry about the plane today, Phil," Lennet said slowly. "Everything happened so fast, I couldn't do a thing."

"It wasn't your fault," Barton responded. "There wasn't anything you could do."

"Won't the insurance money for the lost plane be enough to buy a new one?" Beverly asked.

"When it comes," Barton said. "However, they must investigate and all that takes time. I need a plane now!"

"I'm sure something will turn up," Beverly said encouragingly.

"An optimist!" Philip grinned at her. "I'm

glad I hired you. It is getting late. Why don't you go home?"

"I'm on my way," Beverly responded. "Good night."

She started across the field. Just as she was about to enter her car she noticed that she had forgotten her gloves and turned back. As she re-entered the office she could hear Thelma talking on the telephone. At first the words did not register with Beverly, but when she heard the word "gray," her attention was caught and held.

Thelma was bent over the mouthpiece at the switchboard, speaking in a low voice. She was oblivious to Beverly's presence in the hall, and the young reporter stood silently by the door.

"Yes," Thelma was saying, "that's right— gray! At once! We don't want to waste any time. I'll be here until eight."

Beverly slipped out the door as Thelma finished speaking. The forgotten gloves didn't matter now. Thelma hadn't said much, but the use of the word "gray" bothered Beverly. Had Thelma been using it in a color sense, or had she been using it as the name of a person—and was the person Beverly?

CHAPTER VIII

Followed

ON THE ride back to her hotel Beverly had time to think over the events of her first day with the Barton Airline. She had been accepted by Philip Barton more quickly and easily than she had anticipated, but she was not so sure of Walter Baker and Thelma. Baker harbored the suspicion that she was a reporter. He might have seen her name in the *Tribune* and remembered it. If he ever discovered the truth, there would be plenty of excitement.

As for Thelma—the telephone call Beverly had overheard rankled in her mind. The girl seemed frank and friendly, but at times Beverly had caught Thelma watching her with sharp, speculative eyes.

There was also the pilot, Lennet. Apparently he was a staunch friend of Philip's, but to Beverly's way of thinking he was too often present when something suspicious happened.

Nor could Beverly dismiss from observation Joe Dean, the mechanic employed to keep the airplanes in condition. She had met him and promptly decided that he was harmless to Philip, but now she felt she must reconsider him. Philip had certainly surrounded himself with an odd assortment of characters when he undertook his airline business.

Beverly parked her car and entered the cool, softly lighted lobby of the hotel. She was more tired than she had thought. After a warm bath and a good dinner she would telephone Charlie Blaine and tell him of her progress.

As she waited to step into the elevator a man pushed rudely against her in his haste to get off. He was a short, thin man in a gray suit and hat. She had only a glimpse of his features as he hastened away.

"Are your guests always in such a hurry?" Beverly asked the elevator boy with a smile as they rode up to the fourth floor.

"I never saw him before," the boy answered.

"I picked him up at your floor, but he isn't a guest here. He must have been visiting someone."

The incident forgotten, Beverly entered her room. She had brought the evening paper with her in order to see if there was any mention yet of Barton's missing plane. As she glanced through the paper, one paragraph caught her attention. Counterfeit money was reported to be circulating now in certain midwest cities. It was believed that the bogus bills were originating in the East. Treasury Department agents were on the alert, and an arrest was believed imminent.

Beverly put the newspaper aside and opened her traveling bag, then gasped in dismay. The contents were in dreadful disorder. Hastily she opened the dressing-table drawers in which she had stored some of her things. Those articles, too, were mussed and jumbled. She had not left her things in such condition. Who, then? A curious maid? She ruled out that possibility. The hotel had bonded employees. She found that nothing was missing, so the possibility of a sneak thief was out. Someone had searched her belongings thoroughly but had taken nothing. What had he or she been looking for?

Thelma's telephone call came to her mind

again. Beverly had obligingly given the girl the name of the hotel where she was living. Had Thelma telephoned someone to search Beverly's room? If so, why? What was her motive? Was she seeking a clue to Beverly's real identity?

On the other hand, she had given Philip Barton the name of her hotel, too. Could he have sent someone to search her room?

Puzzled, Beverly took a shower and dressed. Everyone at the Barton Airline seemed to use the excuse of bad publicity and the fear of reporters to discourage strangers, but was that really all it was? To Beverly it seemed that if they were innocent of any connection with counterfeit smugglers, they would welcome investigation in order to prove their innocence.

Beverly smiled to herself when she thought how disappointed the intruder must have been when he found no incriminating papers or letters in her luggage. She was glad she had not tried to use an assumed name. It would have been easier to give herself away then. Since the intruder had failed to discover anything significant in her room, would he leave her alone now?

Beverly enjoyed an excellent dinner in the hotel dining room, and since there was a lingering bit of twilight left she decided to go for a walk and call Charlie Blaine somewhere along the way, before going to bed.

She set out walking slowly, enjoying the unfamiliar city. She always liked new towns, their different architecture, the busy throng on the streets, the lighted shopwindows. She enjoyed her leisurely stroll until she began to become uncomfortably aware of a man pacing behind her. There were always several yards between them, but when she stopped he did also. When Beverly crossed a street he drew closer as though he feared the traffic would hide her from sight. When she quickened her pace he did likewise. She was sure it was the same man who had bumped into her as he was leaving the elevator in her hotel.

Beverly realized that it was unwise to wander about a strange city alone at night, and decided to return to the hotel. However, before doing so, she went into a drugstore to put in her long-distance telephone call to Charlie Blaine. There was a row of telephone booths, all of them empty. Beverly entered one and shut the door. A moment later the man in gray, who had followed her in, entered the booth next to hers. It was obvious that he intended to listen to every word she said.

The booth was far from soundproof. It would never do to telephone Blaine now. Instead, Beverly dialed the number of the Barton Airline. Thelma answered.

"I never asked you what time we start work in the morning." Beverly used the first pretext that came to her.

"Nine o'clock," Thelma answered. "How's everything?"

"Fine," Beverly said, surprised.

"I just wondered if you got home safely," Thelma remarked. "See you in the morning."

"Good-bye," Beverly responded.

She heard the door to the next telephone booth open, and when she emerged the man in gray was hurrying out of the drugstore. When Beverly stepped to the pavement she saw him loitering by a shopwindow next door.

There was no doubt in her mind now. The man was going to follow her until he learned something about her. How could she report to Blaine with this character waiting to hear every word she said? The telephone call would have to wait until she was back in her room.

Beverly turned her steps toward the hotel. She thought once of going up to the man and demanding to know why he was following her. However, she decided that such a direct attack would bring no answer from him and might ruin any chance she had of discovering who had hired him to shadow her.

Beverly entered the hotel and was about to cross the lobby to the elevator when she stopped. She would not even be able to telephone Blaine safely from her room. What was to prevent the man in gray from following her upstairs to listen at her door?

She dropped into a deep armchair to think the matter over. The man in gray lingered by the hotel entrance, almost hidden by a huge potted plant. She could feel his eyes boring into her. This was becoming irksome. She did not intend to be balked in her campaign so easily. Once she talked to Blaine, she might have a surprise for this gentleman in gray.

Talk to Blaine, yes, but how could she do it in privacy? No matter where she went her shadow followed closely. She glanced up and suddenly she smiled broadly. It was the perfect answer. The man in gray would not be able to follow her. There was sure to be a telephone and she could call whomever she pleased without being overheard by him. In another moment she was on her feet and hurrying toward the ladies' lounge.

CHAPTER IX

The Finger of Guilt

"You're doing fine, Beverly," Charlie Blaine told her. "Report to me again tomorrow night. I'll give you the name of a Treasury agent to call on if you need help in an emergency."

Beverly carefully wrote down the name and address Blaine gave her.

"Do you have any definite suspects, Bev?" he asked.

"Right now I suspect them all for one reason or another," she replied.

"Prove it against one of them," he said.

"Even if it is Philip Barton?"

Blaine was silent so long that she thought they had been disconnected.

"Hello!" she said urgently.

"That isn't what I hoped for," Blaine said slowly, "but if it is the truth—"

"I hope it won't be," Beverly declared.

"If you find he's not involved, take any definite clues you uncover to the T-men," Charlie Blaine instructed her. "And if you find he is *innocently* involved, Bev, see what you can do to get him out of it," he pleaded.

When Beverly emerged from the ladies' lounge she looked for the little man in gray. He was still standing by the door so she went to the elevator. She rode up only one floor and then hurried down the stairs to the lobby again. She was just in time to see the man in gray leaving the hotel. She followed him as he went down the street, hurrying along, head bent in thought.

"Now," Beverly thought with satisfaction, "it's my turn! I'd like to know who told you to follow me."

The man turned into the same drugstore in which Beverly had sought to telephone earlier. He went directly to a telephone booth and Beverly imitated his tactics by choosing the booth next to his. She didn't believe he was aware of her behind him, so deep in thought had he been. Straining her ears to catch the sound of his voice through the thin partition, she heard him say:

"I couldn't discover a thing. Yes, she's gone back up to her room. Nothing, I tell you! I'm going back to my hotel. You can reach me there."

Beverly did not stir from the telephone booth until the man was on the street. When she followed he was nowhere in sight. He must have gotten into a taxicab. Disappointed, she returned to her hotel. She had learned nothing. The man hadn't used any names in his telephone conversation, but Beverly had a hunch that it was Thelma to whom he had been talking.

As Beverly crossed the lobby toward the elevator a girl stepped in front of her. She was fair, with direct blue eyes and a deep suntan. Her blue sport dress was well made and very becoming.

"Miss Gray?"

"Yes." Beverly was puzzled.

"I asked the room clerk to point you out to me. I am Susan Trent. I'd like to talk with you for a few moments."

In bewilderment Beverly followed the other girl to two chairs against the wall. She had never heard of Susan Trent. Who was she and what did she want?

They sat down and the blonde girl fingered her

handbag nervously. Her blue eyes studied Beverly with a worried frown.

"Well?" Beverly suggested with a smile.

"Why did you make Phil—I mean, Mr. Barton, hire you this morning?" the girl burst out.

Beverly sat back in her chair. Another surprise! Was this also another suspect?

"I didn't *make* him hire me," she said slowly. "I asked him for a job and he gave me one."

"He doesn't need any more help," the girl said stubbornly. "He has hardly any business. How is he going to pay you?"

"Why don't you let him worry about that?" Beverly asked coolly. "I don't see that it is any business of yours—"

"Oh, but it is," the girl said almost tearfully. "Phil is too trusting. He just keeps getting into more and more trouble."

"I don't want to cause him any trouble," Beverly assured her. "I'd like to help him."

"Why?" the other girl demanded. "Did you know Phil when he lived in New York? Did you follow him down here?"

"I never met him until this morning. I was looking for a job and Mr. Barton gave me one," Beverly said slowly. "I fail to see what there is to worry you in that. I've told you I want to help him, and not to hurt him."

"Too many people have tried to help him. It only makes matters worse," Susan declared. "Why don't you go away and let him alone?"

"How did you find out I was working for the Barton Airline?" Beverly asked. "The news certainly must have traveled fast. I had no idea I would cause such a commotion."

"I talked to Phil on the phone tonight," Susan said.

"And what are you afraid I might do?" Beverly demanded. "Rob the safe or dynamite a hangar—"

"I think any one of those things might happen," the other girl said soberly. "That's about all that hasn't happened to Phil lately."

"I assure you I won't destroy anything," Beverly told her with a smile.

"Prove it by leaving now," Susan urged. "You can get a better job somewhere else."

"I seem to be a definite threat to someone's plans for the Barton Airline," Beverly said thoughtfully. "Everyone is so anxious for me to leave. Well, for your benefit and for the benefit of whoever sent you to talk to me, I am not going to leave until Philip Barton tells me to. You can tell that to your friend in gray, to Thelma Chase, and to Walter Baker."

"No one sent me," Susan Trent said in surprise. "I came to see you, because I hoped—"

"Exactly who are you?" Beverly asked.

"Susan Trent."

"You said that before," Beverly observed, smiling, "but I don't recognize—"

"Perhaps Phil didn't mention my name," Susan murmured.

Beverly recalled Walter Baker's words at lunch: "He is interested in some girl in Miami."

"Are you engaged to Mr. Barton?" Beverly asked.

The other girl nodded. "Yes, but we have kept it a secret because his father would not approve. Once Phil has made a success of his airline and has a definite future, we will be married."

"I hope you weren't jealous of me!" Beverly exclaimed.

The other girl blushed. "I suppose I was—a little, and afraid, too. You see, the airline means so much to both of us—"

"You have nothing to fear from me," Beverly assured her warmly. "I'd like to help you both."

"Why?" the girl insisted. "Why are you so interested?"

"Because I can see that Mr. Barton is doing his best to make a go of it," Beverly said, "and he isn't getting any help."

The girl looked dubious. Then she smiled.

"Phil says he trusts you, so I will too. I'm sorry I bothered you tonight, Miss Gray."

"I'm not," Beverly said. "I'm glad I met you. I hope you and Mr. Barton will have a very happy future together."

Beverly watched the girl leave the hotel and then went up to her room. She slept restlessly, her dreams haunted by counterfeit dollar bills marching in a parade which was led first by Thelma, then by Walter, and then by Philip Barton and Susan Trent.

In the morning she bought a newspaper and took it into the dining room to read while she had her breakfast. After she had given her order she opened the paper. There, staring up at her from the front page, was a picture of the man in gray.

The picture was captioned "Counterfeiter," and the story was that late the previous night the man had been arrested in a downtown hotel. A quantity of counterfeit bills had been found in his luggage. He claimed to have been working alone, but the police did not believe his story and were searching for his accomplices.

Beverly ate her breakfast in record time. If her hunch about Thelma was correct, the girl was one of those accomplices. Even if the police did not succeed in connecting her with the man in gray, Thelma was sure to be upset by his arrest.

The drive along the smooth, flat road crossing numerous little canals, beneath a blue sky dotted with fleecy white clouds moving like lazy ships, was one to be enjoyed at any time of the day, but this morning Beverly had scant attention for it. Her thoughts revolved around the arrest of the man in gray and his connection, if any, with Thelma.

There were two cars parked beside the building when Beverly arrived, and when she pushed open the glass door she found Thelma and Lennet bent over the morning newspaper.

"Anything exciting in the news?" Beverly, who had left her own paper in the car, inquired brightly.

"No, nothing," Thelma answered swiftly. "We didn't expect you so soon."

"An early bird!" added Lennet with a grin.

"I always think it is better to be early than late," Beverly responded. "Any reports about the stolen plane?"

"None," Lennet replied. "It certainly is a mystery."

"Good morning, everyone!" Philip Barton entered. The frown on his face surprised them. "I'd like to talk with you, Lennet."

The pilot followed the other man into the latter's private office and Beverly looked thoughtfully after them. Lennet and Thelma—studying the story of the man in gray. Beverly had just about decided that Thelma and Walter Baker were working together, but now Lennet began to change her mind. Philip, too, was perturbed about something and wanted a secret conference with Lennet. Philip and Lennet—they were the two the Treasury agents had suspected in the beginning. Was it Philip after all?

Beverly stepped out of the building to let the cool morning air clear her muddled thoughts. Every step leading to the counterfeiters seemed to entangle her more and more in a mass of doubts and uncertainty. Despite his weaknesses and irresponsibility, Beverly liked Philip. Somehow, she did not believe he would do anything deliberately dishonest. If counterfeit money was entering the country on his planes she wanted to believe he was ignorant of that fact. Someone was making him a scapegoat and he was too gullible to realize it.

Suddenly Beverly straightened and drew back into the shadow of the building. A man was leaving hangar No. 2, and he obviously did not want anyone to see him. His head bent, he walked rapidly along the side of the hangar, pausing only once to look back over his shoulder to make sure he was not being observed, and then disappeared around a corner of the building. But in that moment Beverly had recognized him. It was Walter Baker.

Beverly hurried to the hangar and opened the door. Nothing seemed amiss. There was no smell of smoke as she had feared there might be. The silver wings of the plane stretched above her like the widespread wings of a poised seagull. She walked about the hangar, reassuring herself that all was as it should be. If destruction should come upon another of Barton's planes, the young man's freight service would be finished.

Puzzled, Beverly went outside again and followed the direction she had seen Baker take. No one was in sight. Why had Walter Baker been sneaking out of the hangar? As bookkeeper, he had no concern with the mechanical end of the airline. Only on rare occasions did he have business in the plane hangars and then there was no reason for him to behave in such a suspicious manner.

Slowly and thoughtfully Beverly went back to the little office building. She was passing the window to Philip's private office when she heard voices within the room.

"I don't like it," Philip was saying. "The fact that they are still in Miami shows they could drop in on us any time."

Beverly stopped to listen, leaning carelessly against the building as if she were merely enjoying the view. She told herself that eavesdropping, no matter how opposed to it she normally was, might supply a clue to further her search for the counterfeiters.

"There is nothing to connect us with the man who was arrested," Lennet said calmly. "What are you worrying about?"

"You would worry too, if your whole future was about to explode in your face," Philip retorted.

"If there is even a breath of suspicion thrown on me now, I'll never get the Allied Farms contract. I'll lose my business and my father will disinherit me for good!"

"No one suspects you of anything," Lennet told him. "We were cleared in the investigation. No one can prove that either one of us is connected with the counterfeiting gang in any way."

"Oh no?" Philip said. "The Treasury agents are still busy in Miami. They might somehow connect my missing plane with the counterfeit money which is being smuggled into the country."

"Impossible!" Lennet exclaimed.

"Why is it impossible?" Philip countered. "You don't know who stole it—do you?"

"No, of course I don't," Lennet said angrily. "But why would the T-men figure an angle like that?"

"I don't know," Philip said heavily, "but I wish I knew what they *are* thinking."

Lennet said encouragingly, "Don't get the creeps, Phil. Well, I'm going out to see if Thelma will have lunch with me today."

There was the sound of a closing door and Beverly cautiously peeped over the window sill. Philip Barton was standing with his back toward her. He pulled something from his pocket and stood staring at it for several long moments. Finally he bent and pushed it far out of sight in his lower left-hand desk drawer. Then he, too, left the office.

What had he been studying so carefully? Beverly wished she could have seen it more plainly. Impulsively she took a quick look around the field. No one was in sight. Then she reached up and caught hold of the window sill. By finding a toehold on the wall, she managed to pull herself up until she could swing over the window sill into Philip's office.

Once inside, she held her breath, listening at the door, before she noiselessly turned the key to make sure she wouldn't be disturbed. Then she went to Philip's desk and opened the lower left-hand drawer. Far back in the corner she found a small, crumpled green ball of paper. She smoothed it out and studied it. She continued to study it until she was sure. It was like the finger of guilt coming to rest at last upon Philip Barton. It was a ten-dollar bill and it was a counterfeit.

CHAPTER X

Sabotage

WHEN Beverly returned to her desk in the office Walter Baker was sitting at his own desk, so busy that he scarcely noticed her. It was hard to believe that only a short while ago he had been acting like a sneak thief.

It was almost noon when Philip Barton entered the office, excitement in his eyes and voice. He leaned over Walter's desk and his words were plainly audible to Beverly.

"We've got the Allied Farms contract, Walter! That ought to pull us out of trouble."

"Fine!" Walter rubbed his hands together in pleased anticipation. "When do we make the first shipment?"

"Monday. I'm going out now and tell Joe to get number two ready."

Philip hurried out of the building, and through the window beside her desk Beverly watched his progress across the field. There was a new swing to his shoulders, and his head was high. The new contract meant that his business had taken a giant step toward survival, and he was elated. If he wanted so much to succeed in his business venture, how could he jeopardize everything by dealing with counterfeiters? Beverly couldn't understand it.

Beverly glanced across the room at Walter Baker. He, too, was watching Philip and as the young man entered the hangar Baker turned back to his desk with a sly, secret smile on his face. Beverly thoughtfully resumed her work, wondering why Baker seemed as pleased as the cat who ate the canary.

About a half-hour later Philip re-entered the office. His elation was gone. In place of his jubilant smile was an anxious frown. He dropped heavily into the chair by Baker's desk.

"We're sunk, Walter! Number two is out of commission. Joe says we won't be able to get new parts from the factory and install them in time to ship for Allied Farms."

"How about number three?" Walter asked.

"Too small," Philip shook his head. "Besides,

I've assigned that to San Joanna to take the place of the one we lost."

"What are you going to do?" Baker asked.

"I don't know."

"Your father—" Baker began.

Philip pounded Baker's desk. "Why is it that everyone wants me to go to my father for more money? My father won't give me another dime, and you know it!"

"Of course you can't appeal to your father," Walter agreed. He patted the young man's shoulder. "We'll think of something."

"Whatever it is, it will have to be done quickly," Philip sighed. He got to his feet and went dejectedly into his own office.

Walter looked after the young man for a moment and then turned his attention to the papers on his desk with what looked to Beverly suspiciously like a sneer. She felt anger rise in her.

"It is a shame about number-two plane," Beverly said as she got up to go to the filing cabinet.

"Hm? Oh, yes, it is," Walter answered coldly.

"Do you think someone might have deliberately sabotaged the plane?" Beverly continued.

"Why do you ask that?" Walter now gave the girl his full attention.

"I thought you might have seen a stranger when you were in the hangar this morning," Beverly replied calmly.

Her words were a shock to him and she was gratified to see a flicker of alarm in his eyes.

"When I—"

"I saw you," Beverly nodded coolly. "Perhaps Mr. Barton would like to talk to you about it."

Even as she spoke Beverly realized that she was acting unwisely. She was making an enemy of Walter Baker. It was visible in his eyes and his voice when he spoke to her.

"I do not know what you hope to learn in your work here, Miss Gray, but we of the Barton Airline do not want a snooper in our midst. I think it is high time Mr. Barton knew the truth about you. I shall tell him immediately that you are a reporter sent here to spy upon him, and we will see which one of us he trusts."

Walter Baker flung down his pencil and strode to Philip's office. Beverly followed quickly. Now she was in a bad spot. If Barton hated reporters as much as Charlie Blaine said he did, she would be dismissed instantly. That would finish her connection with the airline and she never would uncover the counterfeiters.

Walter blurted out his story and Philip listened,

at first unbelievingly and then with growing anger.

"I thought I could trust you," he flung at Beverly. "You did your work well. I suppose you're getting a story ready for the headlines: 'Rich Man's Son Fails Again.' It doesn't matter to you that it only means more trouble for me."

"I'm not getting a story ready for any paper," Beverly denied. "It is true I was once a reporter for the *Tribune* in New York, but now—"

"Now she wants us to believe she is working for practically nothing in this out-of-the-way place just because she loves to be near airplanes," Walter said with cutting sarcasm. "Philip, don't listen to her. Discharge her at once, or tomorrow the papers will all have the story of our difficulties and Allied Farms will cancel their contract before we even have a chance to try to fulfill it."

"If there are people here working against the airline, Mr. Barton," Beverly said, "I am not one of them. When I told you I would like to help you save your airline, I meant it."

"I have a friend on the *Tribune*," Philip said slowly. "I'll telephone him and see if you are telling the truth."

Hostile silence reigned in the small room while

Philip waited for his call to New York to be put through. At last he contacted Paul Thurmond and talked to him briefly.

When Philip replaced the telephone, Walter could not contain himself.

"Well? She is a reporter, isn't she?"

"She was," Philip corrected. "Paul said Charlie Blaine discharged her last week. We owe her an apology, Walter. I'm sorry for this scene, Miss Gray."

Philip apologized, but Walter did not. For a moment he glared at her, his face white with suppressed fury. Then he turned on his heel and without another word strode out and slammed the door behind him.

"He will make a bitter enemy," Beverly murmured.

"Don't worry about him," Philip said. "If he makes trouble for you, tell me about it." Unconsciously his shoulders straightened.

"He may make trouble for you," Beverly pointed out.

"Trouble is something I am getting used to," Philip answered with a wry smile. "It has been keeping me company for quite some time."

"I mean it," Beverly persisted. "Why do you trust Walter Baker so implicitly? Don't you ever question any of his decisions or his financial reports?"

"He has been with me ever since I started here," Philip replied. "He always seems to have the good of the company at heart. I have never seen him so angry as he was today."

"I saw him leaving the hangar of number-two plane this morning when he thought no one else was on the field," Beverly said. "I told him I saw him, and that's what brought on this whole business."

"Walter?" The young man seemed stunned. It was as if a pillar upon which he had been leaning for a long time was crumbling beneath him.

"Yes, Walter!" Beverly said grimly.

"But why?" Philip exclaimed. "Why would Walter want to cripple the line just when we've finally landed the Allied contract? Why, he's offered to put money into the business. He even offered to buy me out once, when things looked pretty hopeless—"

"I don't know why," Beverly admitted, "but it certainly looks as if he grounded that plane for some reason." She watched Philip's face pale as she added, "It's barely possible he's a T-man working under cover."

CHAPTER XI

Blackmail

"WAIT! Don't go!" Philip's voice stopped Beverly as she turned to the door. "I think you're on the wrong track. I want to show you something."

Philip drew a slip of paper from his pocket and handed it to Beverly. "If Walter did put number-two plane out of commission, it's not because he's a T-man trying to prevent the delivery of counterfeit—that's what you're thinking, isn't it?" When Beverly nodded, Philip went on: "Someone is out to ruin me, and this note proves it."

It was an unsigned, typewritten note. The envelope bore a Miami postmark under date of the previous day.

" 'If you want to save your airline,' " Beverly read, " 'be prepared to pay five thousand dollars in cash tonight. Come to the edge of Heyman's Swamp at ten o'clock. Come alone. Say nothing to anyone.' "

In spite of its brevity Beverly felt that the writer of the note meant what he said. If Philip wanted to save his airline—

"Five thousand dollars!" Philip gave a short, bitter laugh. "I couldn't pay five hundred dollars for the best protection in the world."

"When did you receive the note?" Beverly asked.

"It was with the mail Thelma brought in to me this morning," Philip answered. "I don't know what to do," he added in a worried tone. "Certainly I want to save my airline, but I can't afford to pay that kind of money."

Beverly thought of the counterfeit bill hidden in his desk drawer and wondered if he really was being as frank with her as he seemed to be.

"Where is Heyman's Swamp?" Beverly wanted to know.

"It is a dismal place about twenty miles from here," Philip replied. "I wonder if I could borrow some money on my car? If I could pay this fellow something on account and promise to pay the rest in a month or so, he might let my planes alone. Once we begin regular shipments for Allied Farms we should start to make a profit, but if my planes are ruined now—"

"If we could only find out who wrote this note," Beverly said, frowning, "it might clear up the mystery of the missing plane as well."

Philip grinned wryly. "A few months ago it wouldn't have mattered to me what became of the line, but lately, since I've tried to develop it and won a few contracts myself, I've begun to take pride in it. It isn't only that I want to show my father that I'm not as worthless as he thinks. I *like* the airline. Sometimes I think I would be satisfied to devote my whole future to building and expanding it. Besides, there is another reason."

"I know." Beverly smiled. "I met her."

"Susan?" he asked eagerly. "She is a wonderful girl and she has a lot of faith in me. I must make good—for us." Young Barton chuckled. "Sounds funny for me to be talking like a serious businessman!"

"No, it doesn't sound funny at all," Beverly said. "I'm sure if your father knew what—"

"My father is to know nothing of my difficulties," he said quickly. "When there is clear sailing ahead of us, with no worry clouds on the horizon, then I'll go to him and tell him about it."

"May I study the note you received?" Beverly asked, once more turning toward the door of the office.

"Take it with you," Philip said. "It's no good to me—I can't possibly meet the terms. There is no use my going to meet the mysterious writer of the note. I don't have five thousand dollars to give him and that is what he'll expect."

As she walked back to her own desk, Beverly was thinking hard. Five thousand dollars was a lot of money, almost an incredible amount for one whose business showed no profit. Whoever wrote the note could not be familiar with Philip's financial status, and yet—

Why the simple, typewritten note should seem strangely familiar to her, Beverly could not explain. There was something about the alignment of the letters, a crooked letter "l" and an "e" that wrote out of line with the other letters, which made her think she had seen that typing before. Where?

Thelma had a typewriter at her switchboard in the hall. There was one that Walter Baker sometimes used, and there was Beverly's own. If she could get a sample of the typing of each machine and compare them with the mysterious note, she might learn something.

When Thelma, Lennet, and Walter asked Beverly to join them again for lunch she declined with the excuse that Mr. Barton had asked her to rush some work for him. After her co-workers had departed Beverly set about comparing typewriters.

It didn't take long to make sure that Thelma's typewriter was not the one on which the note had been written. The type was entirely different in size. Next, Beverly tried the typewriter Walter Baker sometimes used. That one had irregularities in the letters "o" and "p" which did not show up in the note. Beverly went back to her own desk. The note had not been written on either Thelma's or Walter's typewriter.

"But somewhere I've seen that crooked 'l' and raised 'e' before," Beverly told herself with a frown.

Then her gaze fell upon the typewriter allotted to her use. Could it be? Hastily she inserted a sheet of paper and typed a sentence. There it was —the crooked "l" and lopsided "e." The note had been written on *her* typewriter! If Philip should try to trace the note, as she had done, the trail would lead right to her. Was it only coincidence, or was someone deliberately trying to entangle her in the web of mystery being spun about the Barton Airline?

The fact that it was her typewriter which had been used to type the blackmail note proved that someone here in the company—someone who *did* know its precarious financial position—must have sent the letter. Had it been Thelma? Or Walter Baker? Or the pilot, Hugh Lennet? But all three of them knew Philip couldn't raise that kind of money. And if they were part of a gang smuggling counterfeit into the country on Philip's planes, why would they want to wreck the airline? Because Philip was right. Someone did want to, obviously. Of a fleet of four planes, one had crashed, one had been hijacked in mid-air, a third had been sabotaged, and now the one remaining plane, and probably the buildings as well, had been threatened.

Beverly drew the note from the pocket of her blouse and read it again. Tonight at ten o'clock! The writer of the note would go to Heyman's Swamp expecting five thousand dollars. Beverly strode to Philip's office and knocked on the door.

"Come in," his weary voice bade her. "Oh, it's you, Miss Gray."

"Have you definitely decided not to go to Heyman's Swamp tonight?"

"Yes," Philip said. "I don't have the money. There is no use in my going. I will just have to sit here and wait to see what happens."

"No," Beverly said firmly. "You are going to Heyman's Swamp tonight and I am going with you. I want to meet the writer of the mysterious note!"

THE miles sped away behind them as Philip's car left Miami behind and turned southward. It was a half-hour before the appointed time to meet the writer of the mysterious note in Heyman's Swamp. Philip had picked up Beverly at her hotel, and the two young people were thoughtfully silent as they headed for the mysterious rendezvous.

It was a starlit night with the moon like a huge golden pumpkin in the sky. A faint wind whispered in the fronds of the tall grasses bordering the road and rippled the waters of the narrow canals they crossed. There was little traffic along this highway and only a few isolated houses.

"He certainly picked a remote spot," Beverly

complained as the foliage grew thicker and habitation sparser.

"We're lucky he didn't choose a haunted house," Philip commented with a grin. "This is in the best mystery-story manner, isn't it? In every mystery book I've ever read, the black-mailer always chooses the loneliest spot in town."

"If only it were in town!" Beverly said. "Why didn't he choose a busy street corner instead of making us come away out here?"

"He didn't know you were coming," Philip reminded her, "and if I were you, I would stay hidden in the car until the man shows himself. He told me to come alone. If he learns that I have company he may not appear."

"I'll sit on the floor in the back until you meet him," Beverly agreed.

When they were about a mile from Heyman's Swamp Philip stopped the car in order to let Beverly secrete herself on the floor in the rear of the car. When she was safely curled up on a blanket Philip got back into the driver's seat.

"No one would know you are there," he assured her as he started the car, "and I wish you weren't. We don't know what we are getting into. I wish I hadn't let you come."

"Stop worrying," Beverly said brightly. "Two of us may be able to cope with this mysterious blackmailer where one would be unable to."

"This looks like the spot," Philip said, bringing the car to a halt. "I don't see anyone."

"We better not talk any more," Beverly advised. "He might hear us."

Philip sat behind the wheel of the car, nervously peering first this way and then that. Nothing but black shadows surrounded them. Once a tree branch stirred in the breeze and its moving shadow caused him to think someone was approaching.

"A false alarm," he muttered. "I wish he would come and get this suspense over with."

From her position on the floor Beverly could see nothing but patches of the star-studded sky through the network of tree branches. Night sounds seemed louder than usual. Once a bird twittered close at hand, and far off they heard a dog barking. Time passed slowly and still there was no sound of another car or person.

Beverly shifted her position once to peer over the front seat at the lighted clock on the dashboard. It was half past ten. They had been waiting for thirty minutes.

"I should think for five thousand dollars he might at least have been on time," Philip whispered. "This waiting is getting on my nerves."

Yes, why didn't the blackmailer come, Beverly wondered. Was it possible that he had learned somehow that Philip was not alone and so did not intend to put in an appearance? That was hardly likely. They had moved with the utmost discretion.

"A half-hour!" Philip complained. "I wish I hadn't come!"

"Where would you have been tonight if you hadn't kept this appointment?" Beverly whispered.

"I would have been at the airport to see Lennet take off for San Joanna," Philip replied. "Why?"

"I've been thinking," Beverly answered. "If someone didn't want you at the airport tonight they would try to make sure you were somewhere else. A note such as the one you received this morning would be pretty sure to take you away."

"The airport!" Philip muttered. "Here we go!"

Without further ado Philip started the car and swung it about. They raced along the road, convinced now that the blackmail note had merely been a ruse to lure Philip away from the airport.

"I should have guessed," Philip said. "It is well known in these parts that I haven't any money. It would be foolish for anyone to try to blackmail me. I should have guessed it was a hoax."

"With the things that have been happening at the Barton Airline lately, you can't be sure of anything," Beverly returned. "Besides, it's my fault. I persuaded you to come."

Philip hunched over the wheel and concentrated on his driving. Beverly was glad that there were few curves and hardly any traffic.

At last they approached the Barton field. Philip swung into the parking lot and shut off the motor. Everything was quiet and peaceful. The office building was a dark blotch on the landscape. A light was visible through the window of one of the hangars. The moon slipped from behind a cloud and lighted the field. Nothing stirred anywhere.

"Joe is still working on number two," Philip murmured as he got out of the car.

Beverly followed him across the lot. As they looked through the hangar window they could see the mechanic working at the motor of the plane.

"Hi, Joe!" Philip said as he entered the hangar. "Is everything okay?"

"I hope to have one engine ready to test in the morning," the mechanic replied. "Lennet took off on time and Miss Chase just left."

"Did Thelma work tonight?" Philip asked in surprise.

"Well, she wasn't exactly working." Joe grinned. "She stayed to talk to Lennet until he took off."

"Have you seen or heard anything unusual tonight?" Philip continued.

"No, sir, everything has been quiet," was the reply, and the mechanic turned back to his job.

"It looks as though our fears were for nothing," Philip said to Beverly. "Come on, I'll take you back to your hotel."

"Perhaps you better check the other hangar," Beverly said, still uneasy, "while I look around the office."

"All right. I'll meet you at the car," he agreed.

Philip strode to the hangar which had been occupied by his third plane when it was grounded between flights. Beverly watched him disappear inside and then she turned toward the office.

The light switch was right inside the door and

she snapped it on as soon as she opened the door. The place was just as she had seen it last this afternoon. The desks were undisturbed, typewriters and adding machine covered, telephone silent. The only moving things were the hands on the big clock above the door.

Beverly glanced into Philip's private office and that, too, was undisturbed. She walked to Thelma's switchboard and desk and glanced around. There was no buzzing and no signal light now. Thelma had put everything away. Her corner, for once, was neat and tidy. On the floor was a list of numbers which had missed the wastepaper basket or had been dropped unintentionally. Beverly picked up the slip of paper and studied it for a moment. She dropped it into the basket and then retrieved it again. She had noticed that Thelma had a habit of crumpling papers into a ball before she threw them away. However, this list was smooth and neat. Perhaps it had fallen without her knowledge. Beverly tucked the list into her pocket and turned to see Philip standing in the doorway.

"I thought I'd come after you," he said. "Are you satisfied that everything is all right?"

"Yes," Beverly said, "but I am still puzzled

about the blackmail note. When the man didn't meet you I was sure it was only a ruse to keep you away from here. Now—"

"Now we are going back to town," Philip said. "We will have a sandwich and coffee, and you are not to worry any more. I appreciate your taking all this trouble on my behalf. Why do you do it?"

"I'd like to see the Barton Airline stay in business." Beverly replied, smiling.

"That's what you tell me," Philip said. "But I feel that there is something more behind it. All right!" He held up his hand to interrupt as she started to speak. "I won't ask any more questions. If you don't care to tell me, that is your business. I just want you to know it helps my morale to know there are at least two people on my side."

Beverly was very thoughtful after she said good night to young Barton later that night, and went to her room. Charlie Blaine had sent her down here to try to prove that Philip was innocent of the counterfeit smuggling of which he had been suspected. She had been forced to believe that he was involved when she found the counterfeit bill in his desk drawer. But her reporter's training had long since taught her that a man's motives are best judged through knowledge of his character. And Philip Barton either was a consummate actor or else he simply didn't add up to the kind of person who must be back of the mysterious happenings at the Barton airfield. Beverly decided to reserve judgment on young Barton for a while, in spite of the damaging evidence of the ten-dollar counterfeit in his desk drawer.

And what about the blackmail note? Had it accomplished its sole purpose when it lured Philip away from the airport for a time?

Beverly stood by her open window, and while her eyes watched the city's lights below, her mind tried to fathom the mystery. She was about to accept the theory that counterfeiters were bringing their fake money in on Barton's planes unknown to him; but if so, why would they steal one plane and put a second out of commission? Why would they try to bankrupt the line itself?

"Why!" she exclaimed aloud as she dropped into a chair. She was back to the same illogical factor that had baffled her earlier.

If the counterfeiters depended upon Barton's planes to bring their money into the United States, why try to bankrupt the line? It would be like killing the goose that laid the golden eggs. They needed the planes to further their schemes.

When she considered it from that angle, it knocked her theory to pieces.

"We don't know that they wrecked the plane," she argued with herself. "No wreckage has been found."

If they didn't wreck the plane, then what? Did they hide it? How could anyone hide such a huge thing? Even as she wondered about it she remembered the many small islands and coves of the Florida Keys. A plane could be concealed and camouflaged to avoid detection. The authorities were looking for a wreck. She would like to look for a plane in hiding. To do that, she should have her own plane. It would be impossible to search adequately on short trips by car. From the air she could do so much more in a shorter time. However, it was obvious she couldn't borrow a plane from Philip for the purpose. What to do about it?

"Larry!" she exclaimed aloud. "I'll phone Charlie Blaine and ask him if I can send Larry an S O S to fly down. In Larry's *Red Bird* we will search the whole state of Florida if we have to, until we find Philip's plane!"

girl wanted to be sure Beverly was going where she said she was. "Can I give you a lift into town?"

"Thanks, no," Thelma said. "I have my own car here."

Puzzled by Thelma's latest action, Beverly went out to her car. She pressed the starter button but nothing happened. Time after time she tried, but her car did not respond.

"Having trouble?" Philip came from the airfield.

"I don't know what's the matter." Beverly frowned. "It was running fine when I parked this morning."

"They get temperamental sometimes," Philip grinned. "Let me take a look at the motor." He lifted the hood and peered in at the engine.

"Perhaps I can drive you to town, Beverly?" Thelma spoke behind them.

Beverly glanced at her watch and frowned. It was after one-thirty already. She didn't have much time to get to the theater to meet Larry.

"Yes," she said, "I would be very grateful."

"Go along with Thelma," Philip said. "I'll fix your car for you and leave it at your hotel."

Everything was working out fine, Beverly

thought ruefully, especially for Thelma. The blonde girl drove with a faint, satisfied smile upon her face which irked Beverly. Circumstances apparently had played right into Thelma's hands, and Beverly didn't like it.

"I don't understand about my car," Beverly declared. "I've never had any trouble with it before."

"They all break down once in a while," Thelma said. "I wouldn't worry about it. Mr. Barton will fix it for you."

"If he can," Beverly amended.

"Oh, I'm sure he can," Thelma said cheerily. "Your play is at the Center Theater, isn't it?"

"Yes," Beverly said, "but I don't want to take you out of your way. Drop me anywhere and I'll go on to the theater alone."

"I wouldn't dream of that," Thelma protested. "You might get lost. No, I'll take you to the theater."

Saturday traffic was heavy and progress was necessarily slow, but Thelma bore it all cheerfully.

"There!" she said, stopping directly in front of the theater entrance. "You've plenty of time to make the curtain."

"Thanks a lot," Beverly said, hastening to get out of the car. "See you Monday!"

Thelma calmly sat in the car and waited until she saw the ticket taker accept Beverly's ticket, regardless of the fact that she was holding up traffic and other cars in line were tooting their horns at her. It was as if she wanted to be sure Beverly went into the theater, and she did not intend to leave until she was satisfied. She waved a white-gloved hand as Beverly disappeared beyond the cool, shadowed lobby, and then drove away.

Beverly was chagrined that Thelma had managed to spy upon her so neatly, but she felt triumphant, too, in that she had outwitted the other girl without arousing suspicion.

Beverly followed the usher down the aisle to her seat and found Larry already occupying the one next to hers.

"Now, for goodness sake, explain these mysterious goings on," Larry said when first greetings were over. "Your telephone call last night told me scarcely anything. Why couldn't you meet me at the airport? Why did you leave my ticket at the hotel with a note telling me to meet you at your seat? It sounds like a television serial."

"It is," Beverly laughed, "and this isn't nearly

the last chapter. But I have Charlie Blaine's permission to tell you some of the story, since you are going to help me."

Quickly and clearly she told Larry of the events which had taken place since her arrival in Miami, of her suspicions and plans.

"Ever since the man in gray, I've been afraid someone else might be watching me," Beverly said. "I didn't want anyone to see me meet you. If you are going to help me I don't want them to suspect you. I have hopes that in the *Red Bird* I will be able to find a clue to the missing airplane—"

"*You* will be able to find it!" Larry demanded. "I thought we were partners. Is it me or my airplane you really want down here?"

"Your airplane," Beverly teased, "but where else could I find such a handsome pilot?"

"Here comes the orchestra," Larry said. "Since we saw this show in New York it won't matter if we leave at once. You know the story, if anyone should ask you about it. Where do we start our search? Do I get to meet Philip Barton?"

"Not right away," Beverly answered. "It's funny, I was all enthused about jumping into the *Red Bird* and starting the search at once, but now—"

"Now?" Larry prompted.

"Thelma acted so queerly—as if she wanted to be sure I'd be in the theater all afternoon. I have a hunch she is up to something," Beverly said. "Something that concerns me."

"What do you want to do about it?"

"I think it was Thelma who sent the man in gray to search my hotel room, and since he didn't find anything—"

"You think she may be trying it herself?" Larry asked.

"Let's stop at the hotel and find out," Beverly proposed.

As the house lights dimmed and the curtain rose on the show, Beverly and Larry stole out one of the side exits and hailed a taxicab.

It was only a short ride to the hotel and Larry suggested that while Beverly went up to her room to reassure herself, he would telephone the municipal airport and tell them to refuel the *Red Bird* so that it would be ready when they arrived. He would join her on the street after she came out of the hotel.

Beverly opened the door to her room with misgivings. She had been apprehensive about what she would find, but there was nothing unusual in the scene that met her eyes. She must have been overly suspicious and mistaken about Thelma's actions. Everything was just as she had left it. The bed was neatly made, her dresses hung neatly in the closet, her toilet articles were undisturbed on the bureau.

She was about to close the door and return to the lobby when the telephone rang.

"Miss Gray?" a masculine voice said rapidly. "This is a friend. Take my advice. Leave the Barton Airline at once and never return."

Beverly gasped. Then she said, speaking in a high voice, "I'm sorry, sir. Miss Gray is out. This is the maid."

The line went dead. Whoever it was had hung up. Beverly flew from the room. Not wanting to waste time waiting for the elevator, she dashed down the four flights of stairs and across the lobby to the public telephone booths. Two were occupied by women. The others were vacant. Beverly sighed in exasperation, then turned and walked briskly out of the hotel.

"Whoa!" Larry exclaimed, catching her arm. "What's the rush?" He had been watching for her on the street.

"Someone just telephoned my room and threatened me!" Beverly burst out.

"Was it Thelma?" Larry asked.

"No," Beverly said more slowly. "It was a man. Thelma thinks I am at the theater. It must have been someone else—someone who saw me go to my room. Someone has been waiting for me!"

"Not necessarily," Larry returned. "The call may have come from outside the hotel. Perhaps he tried to reach you several times and only now succeeded. What did he say?"

Beverly repeated the message and Larry frowned.

"Why don't you take his advice before something unpleasant happens?"

"Quit under fire?" Beverly shook her head. "If he only knew it, that is the best way to make me stay with the airline until I find out what is going on. Do you realize, Larry, that I must be on to something? Someone is afraid of me and of what I know or may learn, and he is trying to scare me away. I wonder who it was? Walter Baker? Or Philip Barton himself?"

"Do you still suspect him, too?" Larry demanded.

"Not really," Beverly said, "but I must be sure. He is a nice young man, I think, with an inferiority complex, but I am sure, if he has a chance to really build up his airline, he will change for the better. I rather like him."

"Should I be jealous?" Larry wanted to know.

Beverly laughed. "Of course not! Let's get started on our search."

"Promise me that if you even suspect someone of trying to harm you, you will call me," Larry urged. "I don't like mysterious warnings. They usually are the forerunner of trouble."

Beverly linked her arm in his and started for the door. "They shouldn't mean a thing to old trouble-shooters like us. Let's forget it and get on with the search," she urged.

Larry had chosen to land his plane at a large airport north of the city, and the ride to the field gave Beverly time to acquaint him with more facts about the missing plane and the state of affairs at the Barton Airline.

"Somebody certainly is trying to put Barton out of business," Larry agreed. "If you want to help him, then so do I."

"I knew I could count on you," Beverly said.

"Do you have any searching campaign planned?" Larry asked.

"The hijacked plane was en route from South America," Beverly said. "Lennet claims he was only about fifty miles from the field when it all happened. I hardly think the thief would fly the plane over the city and risk being seen. Therefore, I believe the plane is somewhere south of the airport."

"South of the airport!" Larry whistled. "That could mean all the way down to the equator."

Beverly chuckled. "No! Philip checked on how much fuel Lennet took on at San Joanna. The plane didn't have more than a quarter-tankful when Lennet lost it."

"That narrows the area," Larry nodded. "Have you thought that they may have unloaded the cargo and then deliberately crashed the plane in the sea?"

"That is what everyone seems to think, but I don't," Beverly answered.

"Why not?"

"Because I don't think hijackers would destroy a plane they could use in their business. What would they gain by it? I think they would want to hold onto it and perhaps use it without Philip's knowledge. It is true, isn't it, that the owner in whose name the plane is licensed is responsible for its compliance with all laws and regulations? If the plane were forced down with—well, say with counterfeit money aboard, Philip would be held accountable, wouldn't he?"

"Aha!" Larry said. "That is the mouse in the woodpile!"

"It is only my theory," Beverly replied hastily.

"It is a very good theory," Larry smiled, "and I'm beginning to think I may someday see it in *Tribune* headlines."

The taxi stopped with a jerk, and they got out. The *Red Bird*, Larry's small cabin plane, stood ready and waiting on the runway. Beverly had piloted the little plane many times and had earned her pilot's license with it. Now, as whenever she stepped into a plane, she felt again the thrill of being airborne.

Larry sat at the controls and Beverly took the seat next to him, charts and maps of the coast on her lap. Through the cabin window she watched the field drop away as they climbed into the sun. The sparkle of the fine day was even more apparent up here.

"You love it, don't you?" Larry smiled.

"Flying? More every time!" Beverly nodded.

Larry increased their air speed and pointed to the maps.

"What are the orders, skipper?"

"Along the coast," Beverly said. "The plane must have landed along the shore since the hard sand is about the only place a plane of that size could land safely without attracting the attention of the police."

CHAPTER XIV

Runaway

THE *Red Bird* flew high above the Barton field and along the coast, with two pairs of eyes scanning the earth for some sign of a grounded airplane.

Miles of narrow, white highway wound between groves of citrus fruits in the rich Redlands district south of Miami. They passed over the Parrot Jungle and the Monkey Jungle. They saw numerous fishermen, and once, flying low enough to skim the treetops, they could see fish visible on the sandy bottom of the sparkling water. They spotted boats far out at sea and plenty of bird life along the shore. They saw a great deal of Florida, but they saw nothing that looked like a grounded airplane.

"Maybe my hunch wasn't so good," Beverly sighed.

"We won't give up yet," Larry counseled. "We'll go as low and as slowly as we can. There is one spot on the beach that I'd like to look at again."

"What did you see?" Beverly asked eagerly.

"It wasn't a plane," Larry said hastily, "but it seemed an odd spot for such a building."

The *Red Bird* turned and headed north again. They were flying over a strip of hard beach when Larry pointed below.

"See that down there? It looks like a canvas-covered framework of some kind."

"It is big enough to cover a plane," Beverly said excitedly. "Can we land and inspect it, Larry?"

Larry studied the stretch of beach before he agreed. Gently the *Red Bird* settled earthward. The wheels touched the sand and the plane bounced to a stop, the tail swinging in a wide arc as Larry applied the brakes.

"I hope we'll be able to take off again," Beverly said anxiously.

"There is plenty of room for a plane the size of the *Red Bird*," Larry reassured her. "Let's get out and see what we have found. It certainly is a deserted spot!"

The beach stretched white and empty on both sides of them. To their back was the rolling surf, and before them was a stretch of tangled foliage at the edge of which sprawled a wide, tentlike affair which once had been camouflaged with tree branches. However, the wind had disturbed the branches and most of them had separated, leaving the canvas plainly visible. There was no other human being within the range of their vision.

"It is like being on a deserted island," Beverly said. "I wonder who built that shed?"

Larry made no reply. Instead, he walked to the shelter and pulled aside a portion of the canvas. Then he beckoned to Beverly excitedly.

"Behold our buried treasure!"

"The plane!" Beverly said in an awe-stricken whisper.

The two young people entered and gazed upward at the wingspread of the silver plane which had once been part of Philip's fleet.

"Look," Beverly said, "someone has painted over the identification numbers."

"They are still faintly visible," Larry pointed out. "Do you recognize them?"

Beverly nodded. "It is Philip's plane all right! I'm going inside the cabin."

Suiting action to her words, Beverly ran to the cabin door. With Larry's help she climbed inside. The freight which had been en route from San Joanna when Lennet lost the plane was still intact. The pilot's charts and maps were undisturbed on the pilot's seat. On the floor was a package wrapped in plain brown paper. Beverly reached for it and looked inside.

"Larry, look!"

"Money!" Larry exclaimed with a whistle.

"Counterfeit, I'll bet!" Beverly replied. "Now the question is, was Lennet carrying it on the plane, or was it put here by the man who stole the plane?"

"We won't know that until we catch the counterfeiters," Larry answered.

"I want to check some of the serial numbers with that list of figures I found by Thelma's board," Beverly went on, taking her copy of the list from her handbag. "Call off a few, will you, Larry?"

Larry complied, but it soon became clear that these numbers did not correspond with the ones on Thelma's list. Beverly sighed.

"If the serial numbers had corresponded, that would have been a definite tie-up between Thelma and Lennet," she said. She sat silent, thinking. "If it was Lennet who was guilty of hiding the plane, I don't think he would have left the money here," Beverly decided finally. "He must have told the truth about losing the plane."

"Whoever took it has been careful with it," Larry commented. "It would be an excellent way to make a fast getaway from these shores."

"For the counterfeiters, you mean."

"Yes. Now that we've found it, what shall we do with it?" Larry wanted to know. "Report it to the police?"

"We should," Beverly said slowly, "and of course we'll have to turn in the counterfeit money right away. But if we tell where we found it, they'll pick up Philip Barton immediately. I—I'll mail the counterfeit to the agent Charlie Blaine told me about, but I'd like to keep the plane a secret for a little while longer. This might make an excellent trap."

"I'll remove a small engine part to make sure no one takes the plane without our knowledge," Larry offered.

Beverly waited impatiently while Larry completed his work. Then they carefully removed all traces of their presence near the plane and returned to the *Red Bird*.

"I wish you would take me back to town and then go to Philip Barton and ask him for a job," Beverly said. "He hasn't any pilots now, except Lennet, because he couldn't afford to keep any idle men on the payroll. Once he knows he will have this plane in time to meet his shipment for Allied Farms, he will need another man in a hurry. I am hoping he will give the job to you— in case we haven't solved the mystery before Monday."

"You definitely suspect Lennet now?" Larry asked.

"If he is the counterfeiter, it would have been wise for him to hide the plane in order to have it for a quick escape, should it become necessary. The fact that the counterfeit money was left in the plane puzzles me. I'm sure he wouldn't be that careless."

"What are your immediate plans, Miss Sherlock?"

"After you talk to Philip I don't plan any action until tomorrow," Beverly said.

"Then we have a date for a turtle steak and

some lime pie," Larry said. "A friend of mine recommended a boat club near Key West. We will fly down tonight where we can dine without any of your suspicious characters spying on us."

"But—" Beverly began doubtfully.

"Everyone gets an evening off now and then," Larry said. "As your fiancé, I demand some of your attention."

"Very well." Beverly smiled. "Telephone me after you talk to Philip Barton."

Beverly returned to the hotel to shower, dress, and wait for Larry's call. She mailed the package of counterfeit money to the Treasury agent whose name and address Blaine had given her, but put no return address or note of explanation with it. She also talked long-distance to Charlie Blaine and reported the latest developments. It was growing dark when Larry telephoned and she went down to meet him outside the hotel.

"Philip didn't hire me, because he doesn't know yet that he's going to need me," Larry reported, "but he has my telephone number and he has promised to call me if his present pilot should be taken ill or an emergency should arise."

"That is good enough," Beverly said. "Once he gets his missing plane back, he is sure to keep you on to fly his shipments for Allied Farms."

The evening was a very pleasant change from others in the past week. Determinedly, Beverly and Larry put suspicions and doubts behind them and enjoyed their air trip, a short taxi ride, a leisurely dinner, and dancing.

The boat club Larry's friend had recommended for unusual food was situated in a quaint village where the chief interest centered in fishing and things of the sea. The club dining room was decorated with sparkling, sequined fishing nets, colorful sea shells, and starfish. The theme of everything was nautical and charming.

"Shades of the *Susabella!*" Larry said, smiling. "We are just a couple of old salts. We can't get away from life on the ocean waves."

"I wonder how all our friends are," Beverly mused. "I miss them. I wonder if they have left Hawaii?"

"Lenora would love this job," Larry declared. "Bev," he said suddenly, "that man at the table by the wall has been staring at you. Do you know him?"

Beverly turned to gaze in the direction Larry indicated, and felt an unpleasant shock.

"It is Walter Baker," she said. "I wonder what he is doing here?"

"Maybe you'll find out," Larry whispered. "He is coming over."

"Good evening, Miss Gray," Walter greeted her stiffly. "You are quite a distance from Miami. I see you have already met the young man who applied for a job late this afternoon."

Beverly smiled. "Yes. Did you come here for a turtle steak, as we did?"

"I'm down for some week-end fishing," Walter replied. "It is time for me to meet my friends. Good night, Miss Gray. Have a pleasant evening."

"I didn't recognize him," Larry confessed when Walter had gone. "Of course I only got a glimpse of him out at the field."

"Pleasant evening!" Beverly grumbled. "Just the sight of him spoiled it. He's up to something."

"Why?" Larry shrugged. "If he wants to go fishing he might very well come to a place like this."

"The first day I worked in the office, he and Thelma took me to lunch," Beverly said slowly. "From one of the remarks he made that day, I assumed that he loathed fishing."

"I see what you mean." Larry frowned. "Well, he has gone now. Shall we dance or go out for a walk?"

"Let's take a walk," Beverly proposed. "Maybe the sights will help us forget him."

"If you wanted to keep the fact that we know each other a secret, it is too late now anyway," Larry pointed out as they strolled along one of the narrow streets leading to the wharves. "Was it his voice that gave you the warning on the telephone?"

"It might have been," Beverly said. "He could have disguised it."

"Then he must be one of the counterfeiters," Larry pointed out.

"Look!" Beverly suddenly drew back into the shadow of a protecting doorway.

A few feet away, in the feeble yellow light from a small shopwindow, stood Walter Baker.

"Waiting for someone," Larry guessed in a whisper.

"Maybe this is a break for us," Beverly said excitedly. "If we can learn whom he is meeting—"

"Shsh!" Larry warned as the man they were watching turned suddenly to gaze in their direction.

Apparently satisfied when he saw no one, Walter turned to examine the fishing tackle displayed in the shopwindow.

"I wonder what he is really doing down here,"

Beverly mused again. "I know he is up to something."

"I'll follow him and report to you what he does," Larry offered.

"Oh no," Beverly objected, smiling. "*We'll* follow him. I'm working on this, too, remember?"

"It is still a partnership," Larry grinned. "Come on, then. Our man is getting fidgety."

A mist was rolling in from the sea. Soft clouds of fog drifted over the street. Walter kept glancing at his watch in the light from the window and peering up and down through the swirling mist. Whoever had an appointment with him was very late.

Suddenly they heard footsteps approaching and Beverly and Larry drew farther back into the shadows. Walter waited expectantly and a moment later a huge man, in a short seaman's coat, and bareheaded, joined him in the circle of light.

"It is about time you got here," Walter growled.

"It was the fog, mate," the man answered cheerfully. "What's the good word?"

"The word isn't so good," Walter retorted. "Where can we go to talk?"

"How about the *Mary B.?*" the man suggested. "We can talk to your heart's content in my cabin."

"Let's get on with it," Walter said impatiently. "I haven't much time."

The seaman turned and started down the street, Walter hurrying beside him.

"C'mon!" Beverly's hand slipped into Larry's. "This may be the break I've been waiting for."

The seaman walked with a rolling gait, as if he were strolling the deck of a plunging ship. His big figure was easy to distinguish through the clouds of mist, and Beverly and Larry had no difficulty keeping their quarry in sight. They followed the two men along the waterfront where numerous fishing vessels and other small craft lay shrouded in fog, the black water lapping gently against their ghostlike hulls, until Walter and his companion turned onto a narrow dock where a long white schooner rode at anchor.

"I'll bet he can take that boat where a good many boats wouldn't dare venture," Larry commented to Beverly as they neared the schooner.

"It should carry a lot of fish," she replied.

"Yes, if it is fish it carries," Larry returned.

Walter and his companion went across a narrow gangplank and disappeared into the cabin of the boat. Beverly and Larry stood in the mist and contemplated the craft.

"There doesn't seem to be anyone else on

board," Beverly whispered after several moments of silence. "I'm going to follow them."

"But Bev—" Larry protested.

"Faint heart ne'er won good story," Beverly misquoted with a chuckle.

Together they negotiated the gangplank and paused on the narrow deck, listening and waiting for discovery, but it did not come. They approached the door to the deck cabin, and Beverly put her ear against the panel. It was too thick to hear what went on inside. Then Larry pointed to a porthole which was open a fraction of an inch. Beverly nodded and they crept close to it. Stealthily Larry's hand went up to push the window open farther. They were rewarded with the murmur of voices as the men inside seated themselves and began their conversation.

"They are growing impatient," the seaman was saying in his gruff voice. "They want action."

"And they shall have it," Walter assured him. "However, this is something that can't be hurried. I thought the end was in sight, but lately there have been new obstacles in my path. You can assure them that I will make the first trip next week."

"Are you sure? We don't want another disappointment. It is too risky for the *Mary B.* now."

"You are being well paid," Walter said dryly. "And you haven't lost your precious boat yet."

"Make sure that I don't," the seaman said. "If the Coast Guard saw us—"

Larry's hand closed warningly on Beverly's shoulder. Footsteps were coming along the deck. A thunderous voice spoke behind them.

"Who might you be? What are you doing on board the *Mary B.*?"

"Run!" Larry whispered in Beverly's ear, giving her a push in the direction of the gangplank while he turned his attention to the sailor who had discovered them.

Quickly and expertly Larry's fist shot out, taking the sailor unaware. It sent him sprawling on the deck and by the time he regained his feet Larry and Beverly were across the gangplank and disappearing in the fog on the dock.

"Whew!" Larry gasped as they ran through the narrow streets. "That was close!"

"He would have to see us just when we were about to learn something!" Beverly complained. "I wanted to know why they have to be afraid of the Coast Guard."

"Wouldn't you be afraid of them if you were a smuggler?" Larry demanded. "I guess we can slow down now. I don't hear anyone coming."

"But I had it all figured differently," Beverly sighed as they found a taxi and started back to the airport. "I thought the smuggler was Lennet. Being a pilot, he had more opportunity."

"This is like riding on a merry-go-round," Larry commented. "As soon as we get settled on one suspicious character, another pops up to change the picture."

"There is one you haven't met yet," Beverly reminded him. "Her name is Thelma."

"The dizzy blonde?" Larry asked. "I met her at the airfield this afternoon."

"But she was off this afternoon," Beverly said, surprised. "She drove me to the theater where I met you."

"Maybe she did," Larry returned, "but when I went out there to talk to Barton, she was there. She asked if he had heard when Lennet was due back."

"What did Philip say?"

"Barton told her Lennet was due about noon tomorrow. Bev, do you really think she is mixed up in it, too?"

Beverly nodded. "I definitely do."

"She seems harmless," Larry commented.

"A pretty face—" Beverly began laughingly.

"Yours is the only pretty face I am interested

in." Larry grinned. "But she did give me a ride into town in her car."

"I hope you were discreet and didn't tell her why you are in Florida," Beverly said teasingly.

"She asked me several leading questions," Larry confessed. "What made me apply for a job at the Barton field? Had I ever met Mr. Barton before? Where did I come from?"

"See?" Beverly exclaimed triumphantly. "She wants to check up on everyone who comes to the field. I went through the same cross-examination."

"It is only natural that she is interested in a new employee," Larry protested. "It might not mean anything."

"I think it does," Beverly insisted. "You choose your suspects and I'll keep mine."

When they got to the airport the fog was lifting, and upon inquiring about weather conditions ahead, Larry was told that Miami was clear.

"I asked Barton if I could land at his field tonight," Larry said as they boarded the plane.

"He won't have any landing lights," Beverly pointed out.

"Yes, he will," Larry told her, "because he said several planes will be using his strip tonight for refueling. Some deal he made with another line, I guess."

The short flight to the Barton field was pleasant and uneventful. They left the fog behind and the moon was full and bright. The airfield was like a silver blanket upon which the *Red Bird* came to rest easily and gently.

"How are we going to get back into town?" Beverly asked. "Philip Barton will have driven my car in to the hotel."

"By bus," Larry said cheerfully. "It won't take long and—"

"Larry, look! There is a light in the office. That is strange. Joe Dean hardly ever goes in there."

"Let's peep in at 'em," Larry whispered, motioning toward a window where the shade wasn't all the way down.

Stealthily, like the two conspirators they were, Beverly and Larry stole up to the office building and pressed close to the window.

"I don't see any—" Larry began in a puzzled tone.

"Shsh!" Beverly warned.

It was then that a figure moved into their range of vision.

"Thelma!" Beverly exclaimed under her breath. "She must have heard our motor when we came in."

"She's probably been hearing planes all evening," Larry reminded her. "Does she live here at the airport?" he demanded. "She spends an awful lot of time here. What on earth is she doing now?"

There was an open leather briefcase on Thelma's desk and she was meticulously removing things from her desk drawer, sorting them, and putting the ones she wanted into the briefcase. The others she destroyed.

"She is going to run away," Beverly guessed.

"It looks that way," Larry said. "But why? She hasn't done anything—yet."

"Nothing we can prove," Beverly replied. "Perhaps the biggest deal is yet to come and she wants to be ready. She might also think there are too many strangers coming to the Barton Airline."

"Meaning you and me," Larry murmured.

In silence they continued to watch Thelma as she cleaned out her desk and packed the briefcase. When she had finished, she turned off the lights and let herself out. Beverly and Larry crouched in the shadow of the building while the girl walked to her car and drove off.

Beverly consulted her wrist watch.

"Hurry, Larry. It is almost time for the bus and we don't want to miss it."

"I can't get over that Thelma!" Larry said, shaking his head.

All during the ride to town Beverly speculated about Thelma and where she was going. Beverly's first impulse had been to stop the girl somehow, but now she began to plan. It was her confident belief that Thelma was in some way in league with Lennet, and in that case she would hardly leave town without seeing him again. He would not land until noon of the following day, so Beverly felt that it would be worth while to see how Thelma spent her time until noon tomorrow.

CHAPTER XV

On the Trail

SHORTLY after eight o'clock the next morning Beverly got into her car, which Philip had left in the hotel garage, and drove to the apartment house where Thelma lived. She parked a short distance away and settled down to wait. Lennet was flying in from San Joanna today, and Beverly had a hunch that he and Thelma would meet before the plane landed at the Barton field. Beverly wanted to see what took place at that meeting.

She had been waiting only about ten minutes when she was surprised to see Thelma come out of the house and get into her car. She must have been very confident that no one suspected her of anything, because she did not notice the car that followed her at a discreet distance all the way across town.

When they came to the open highway Thelma's car put on a burst of speed. Beverly wished now that she had asked Larry to accompany her when she followed Thelma, but she had been afraid two people might be noticed where one might follow undetected.

They drove for more than an hour at a steady speed, and then Thelma suddenly turned her car off the highway onto a narrow dirt road. Beverly stopped her car at once and backed up until the car was hidden from Thelma's sight by a curve in the road. Then she went down the road on foot until she could secrete herself in the tall grass and watch Thelma on the beach below.

It was a lonely stretch of coastline. There was no human habitation for miles. Stiff-legged cranes stalked amid the whispering grass. The trade winds swept in clean and undeterred from the ocean. It was a scene devoted to nature. The cars and the waiting girls were out of place.

Beverly was afraid to stir from her seclusion lest Thelma see her. As it was, a white crane insisted on staring at her with intent, bright eyes.

"Go away!" Beverly implored in a whisper. "I'm sorry if I'm invading your privacy. I'll leave soon, I hope, so please don't give me away."

The bird walked slowly around her, as if wanting to view from every angle this intrusion upon his private world. Finally he went away and Beverly breathed easier.

Time passed slowly and uncomfortably for Beverly. She could see Thelma sitting in her car. Was she impatient too? Every passing minute increased Beverly's danger of being discovered. She wished something would happen soon. Would someone come from the sea to meet the blonde girl? Would Thelma's accomplice come by car on the lonely highway, or—

Even as the thoughts passed through her mind Beverly saw Thelma get out of the car and scan the sky southward. She had a rendezvous here on this lonely stretch of beach with an airplane! Beverly's heart beat faster in excitement. Now she would learn what she wanted to know. Thelma returned to her car and there was another long period of waiting unrelieved by any sign of an airplane.

Beverly was feeling hungry and thirsty and cramped from her crouched position. If only something would happen! The sun on his march across the heavens was pouring noonday heat upon the world, adding to her discomfiture.

Again Thelma got out of the car to search the

sky and consult her wrist watch. For a time she paced up and down the beach. It seemed hours since she had first stopped here. With each passing minute she appeared to grow more impatient and nervous. At last she returned to her car and Beverly heard the motor start.

Beverly remained hidden until Thelma's car passed her and then she ran to her own auto and followed down the highway. As if possessed by anger or anxiety, Thelma drove at high speed through the peaceful countryside. Once she stopped at a wayside lunch stand, but there was a sign posted on the door which read "Closed Sunday," so she continued on her way.

Both cars were proceeding at a fast pace when a brown dog which had been trotting at the side of the road decided to cross the highway. He stepped onto the road, but a blast from Thelma's horn sent him scurrying back to safety. He gazed after the car that flashed past him, then presently stepped onto the road again, oblivious of the fact that a second car was bearing down upon him.

Beverly swung the steering wheel hard to the right as she applied the brake. The dog raced off and disappeared while the car skidded off the road and came to a stop.

When she could catch her breath, Beverly looked down the highway. Thelma had disappeared. Even as Beverly hurried to start her car and get back on the road, she had no real hope of catching the other girl. Thelma might choose any one of a half-dozen crossroads. She was gone, and so was Beverly's hope of an early solution to the mystery.

On the way back to town Beverly decided to stop at the airfield and see if Lennet had landed on schedule. In addition, she hoped to find another clue to Thelma's activities. The girl might have overlooked something when she cleaned out her desk the previous night.

When Beverly pushed open the door to the airline's office she was surprised to see the rest of the Barton employees gathered there.

"Hi!"

Philip Barton was seated on a corner of Thelma's desk while the blonde girl sat at the switchboard and Walter Baker lounged by the window.

"A young man has been frantically telephoning here for the last hour wanting to speak with you. I think he has just about decided that I've spirited you away to an unknown land," Philip told her.

Larry! Beverly smiled.

"Thanks, I'll call him."

"I didn't know I had such ambitious employees," Philip continued. "Sunday morning, the ideal time for a late breakfast in bed, and here we are. Walter was the first one here. I hardly got over the shock of seeing him when Thelma arrived, and now you, Miss Gray. What's the idea?"

"Personal business brought me back to town unexpectedly last night," Walter said. "Since I had a few hours free, I thought I might as well finish up some work I left yesterday."

"Me, too," Thelma chimed in. "I have plenty of typing to do."

"Lennet is the only one missing," Beverly observed, smiling. "Hasn't he landed from South America?"

"He radioed that he had engine trouble and will not get in until tonight," Philip replied.

"Serious trouble?" Beverly asked.

"He didn't say," Philip returned. "I hope it wasn't another trick of our jinx."

"There isn't any jinx," Beverly said firmly. "I think you will soon find that your troubles are due to a very human agency."

With that announcement she left the office and walked out onto the airfield. Philip hurried after her as she had hoped he would.

"What did you mean by that remark?" he demanded. "Miss Gray—Beverly—what have you discovered?"

Beverly looked him squarely in the eye.

"Maybe I shouldn't do it this way," she said, "but I am going to ask you a question and I want an honest answer."

"Shoot!" he said. "My life is an open book."

"Where," asked Beverly, watching his face keenly, "did you get the counterfeit ten-dollar bill that is in your lower left-hand desk drawer?"

Philip turned pale under his tan, but his eyes did not waver under her scrutiny.

"So you know about that," he said heavily. "You won't believe me, any more than the Treasury agents would believe me, but that bill was sent to me in the blackmail note I showed you."

"It was!" Beverly exclaimed. "I wish you had told me then."

"How could I?" Philip shrugged. "If you or anyone else around here had found counterfeit in my possession, how could I be sure you wouldn't report it to the Treasury men? And that's just about all they would need," he added despairingly.

"I think that is just what someone intended to have happen," Beverly said slowly. "There is more than one way to put a man out of business. Philip," she added impulsively, "I want you to trust me. I want you to give me that ten-dollar bill and let me send it to the proper person. I won't involve you, believe me."

Philip Barton looked long into the steady dark eyes confronting him before he said quietly, "I do believe you, Beverly. Come on, I'll get it for you."

They walked back to Philip's office together. He closed the door behind them before taking the telltale bill from its hiding place. Philip then handed the money to Beverly.

"Here it is," he said wryly. "My fate is in your hands."

Beverly folded the bill away in her compact. Then they left Philip's office by the field door. When they were out of earshot of the office building, Beverly said:

"I'm convinced that counterfeiters have been and are still using your planes to smuggle fake money into the country."

"Still?" Philip questioned. "Have you any proof?"

"Yes, and I think I will have more before the day is over," Beverly replied firmly.

"Is—is it Lennet?" Philip queried uneasily.

"Why Lennet?" Beverly asked.

"He acts so funny every time I say anything about the time we were questioned about the counterfeit money," Philip returned.

"Why couldn't it be Walter Baker?" Beverly asked, thinking of the episode on the *Mary B*.

"Walter? He isn't daring enough," Philip said, smiling. "He sits and worries over his books like an old mother hen."

"He worries about his books all right," Beverly retorted, "but I'm not sure that it's your business he's worrying about. Maybe they are working together. Walter may be the leader of the gang, while Lennet actually brings the money in by plane."

"I don't think so," Philip objected. "Haven't you ever noticed how they avoid each other? Lennet is too brash to please Walter."

"It has to be one or the other," Beverly observed, frowning. "From now on, it's just a matter of getting proof."

"Is there anything I can do to help you get it?" Philip asked quickly.

"Yes," said Beverly. "Stay at the airport, and after Lennet arrives, don't let him out of your sight. I am going to work from another angle.

Maybe, between us, we can solve this mystery."

"Good luck," Philip called as Beverly left him and walked off toward her car.

Beverly waved a hand and climbed into the car. On the horn button in the center of the steering wheel was a note. It had been hastily and crudely printed on a sheet of typewriter paper, but its message was plain.

"This is your last warning," she read. "Leave the Barton Airline and do not return." It was signed "A friend."

A FRIEND! Beverly smiled to herself. Was the mysterious friend's name Walter Baker or Thelma Chase? It could only be one or the other. Each had had the opportunity to put the note in her car while she was talking to Philip Barton in his office.

Beverly folded the note and put it into her handbag. The last warning! Leave the Barton Airline—or else! Or else what? Someone had been alarmed by her parting shot as she left the office. She wished she could be sure which one it was.

At that moment both Walter and Thelma came out of the building and got into the latter's car. Neither of them gave any sign that they were aware of Beverly sitting in her car watching them.

Thelma started the car and turned onto the highway in the direction of Miami. After a few moments Beverly followed. She was in sight of
Thelma and her companion nearly all the way to
the city. There, instead of turning in the direction
of Thelma's home, as she had expected them to
do, the pair drove toward the crowded downtown section. Beverly was puzzled. What were
they up to now?

Storage buildings and warehouses loomed
around them. All of the buildings appeared to be
unoccupied, but it was before one of these that
Thelma stopped. Walter got out of the car and
disappeared into the low, sprawling building as
Thelma drove off. Which one should she follow
now? Beverly decided to see what Walter was
doing in the warehouse. This might be an important development in the case. What had
brought him here? Perhaps he was meeting another member of the counterfeiting gang. Beverly decided to take a chance.

She stopped her car and got out. The street
was empty of passers-by. Rapidly she walked to
the warehouse and tried the door by which she
had seen Walter enter. It yielded to her touch and
swung inward on rusty hinges. Dampness and

shadow greeted her. Then she heard receding footsteps and quickly stepped inside.

The footsteps were at the back of the building, and on tiptoe she hastened along the shadowy corridor in order not to lose her quarry. She turned a corner so abruptly that she almost gave herself away. Walter had stopped to open a door to a flight of stairs leading down to the cellar. He hesitated only a moment before he disappeared from her sight.

Beverly allowed several moments to elapse before she approached the door and opened it. Straining her ears to catch the slightest sound, she waited before descending into the darkness. She could hear and see nothing, but her curiosity forced her onward. She went down the stairs slowly, stopping often to listen and wait. Gradually she could see the empty basement. Sunlight struggled through a dirty windowpane at the front of the building, providing the only light in the place. What had happened to Walter?

Then she saw a door in the back wall and walked toward it. She listened first and then lifted the latch. She stepped into a small room which proved to be empty. She was about to retrace her steps when the door slammed behind her. She pulled at the latch in vain, and then she heard a chuckle on the other side of the door.

"Let me out of here!" she demanded angrily.

There was no reply. Whoever it was who had locked the door upon her had gone away. Again and again she tried the door, but no amount of pushing or tugging would budge it. The building was old, but it was solidly built and in good repair. The only other means of egress was a window, high up near the ceiling, and that was protected by an iron grating on the outside.

If it was Walter who had locked the door, and it must have been he, Beverly wondered what it was that had made it imperative to have her out of the way. How long must she stay here? Did anyone ever visit an empty warehouse? Must she wait until Walter decided to return and free her?

Chagrin and anger flooded through her— chagrin at the ease with which she had been trapped, and anger that she had been so stupid as to let herself be tricked in such a manner. She must get out of here! There was an account to be settled with Walter and an airplane to meet with Thelma!

If she shouted, would anyone hear her? It was Sunday, and business places and warehouses were empty of employees. There was scarcely any traffic in the street. She decided to try it, anyway. Her voice echoed back to her from the four walls, but other than that nothing happened. Again and again she tried, and each time silence closed heavily around her. Though her efforts went unrewarded, she kept shouting. There was nothing else to do. She was discouraged and hoarse and about to give up when she suddenly heard an answering shout, and the latch on the door to her prison rattled under someone's hand.

"Beverly! Are you in there?"

"Yes, oh, yes! Open the door!" she cried.

"I can't—there is no key!"

The man on the outside rattled the latch uselessly. Then there was the jar of weight being thrown against the door panel but without result.

"We'll try the window," the man called.

Silence settled down again and Beverly waited impatiently. At last she saw the iron grating lifted aside and the window swung inward. Young Philip Barton thrust his head in and grinned at her.

"Lucky for you that I followed your car."

"I'll be luckier still if you can get me out of here," Beverly declared.

"I've got a rope in my car," he said. "I'll get it and have you out in a jiffy."

He disappeared, and soon a strand of rope spiraled down the wall toward her.

"Hold fast to the end and I'll pull you up," Philip directed.

The ascent was accomplished quickly, with only a skinned knee and a scratched hand as souvenirs of the adventure.

"What happened to Walter Baker?" Beverly asked as soon as she stood in the fading sunlight beside Philip. "I followed him in. Did you see him come out?"

Philip looked blank. "Walter? Not a sign of him."

Beverly gave him a searching glance. Was he trying to protect Walter? No. The ten-dollar counterfeit Philip had entrusted to her was proof that he was innocent.

"Didn't you see anyone?" she asked.

Philip shook his head. "I got separated from you at the traffic light down there. When I got here you were just slipping into the building. I waited in my car for you to come out. When you didn't appear, I began to get worried and decided to look for you."

"Are you sure you didn't see anyone come out?" Beverly insisted.

"No one," Philip answered.

"Then he may still be in the building," Beverly said.

Again Philip disagreed.

"I went all through the place looking for you. There wasn't a sign of anyone. He must have left by another door."

Beverly was forced to admit that Walter Baker had given them the slip.

"I thought you were going to wait at the airport to meet Lennet?" she queried.

"I was," Philip nodded, "but he isn't due for three hours yet, and I was worried about you. When I saw you speed off after Thelma and Walter I thought you might need help, so I followed you."

"I'm glad you did." Beverly smiled. "I wouldn't have wanted to spend the night in that cellar—with probably a dozen rats for company."

"What do we do now?" Philip asked.

"I think you'd better go back to the airport and wait for Lennet," Beverly said. "Don't do anything to arouse his suspicions, but try and learn if he brings any counterfeit money off the plane with him. I'll telephone you later."

"Where are you going?"

"I have a date—with a white crane in a field of grass." Beverly laughed. "See you later!" She waved gaily as she ran to her car and got in.

Soon she was driving through town toward the open highway she and Thelma had followed that morning.

The sky was darkening rapidly. Beverly was afraid that in the shadows she might not be able to find either the right spot or Thelma, but the promise of a moon eased her anxiety. She made one brief stop to telephone Larry at his hotel, but there was no answer, so she left a brief message for him. She hated to make him worry but she felt she could not spare the time to try to find him. If her reasoning was correct, Thelma had a rendez-vous on that lonely beach, and Beverly did not intend to miss it.

When Beverly reached the spot where Thelma had parked that morning, it was deserted. For a moment her confidence wavered. She might be mistaken in the belief that Thelma would return to keep her appointment. Beverly would have to take the chance and wait. She drove beyond the spot and secreted her car as best she could. In the darkness it would not easily be seen. Then she returned on foot to wait near the narrow road onto which she hoped the other girl would drive.

She had been there about twenty minutes, and darkness was complete, when she heard a car coming. A huge, golden moon hung low on the horizon and in a short time the beach would be painted with its light. It would be excellent for Beverly's purpose. The headlights of Thelma's car found the narrow road and turned into it. Thelma stopped the car and got out. She walked slowly down to the beach and sat down. Beverly breathed easier now. So far, her hunch had been right.

The moon ascended the heavens and the beach became a strip of milky whiteness against the water. Thelma continued to sit and gaze out across the ocean. Time passed slowly and Beverly felt on fire with impatience. Then she saw Thelma get to her feet. There was a faint hum to be heard, increasing in volume until the sweep of wings, low in the sky, came directly toward them.

Beverly was afraid to move for fear she would attract the attention of the pilot as he circled overhead preparing to land. As soon as she was sure that neither the pilot nor Thelma would be watching, Beverly hastened nearer, bent low, shielding herself in the tall grasses that plucked at her dress and tangled themselves in her hair.

The plane settled heavily on the hard, level beach, and rolled to a stop a few feet from where Thelma was waiting. Through the glasses she had brought from the car, Beverly could identify the plane as the one from the Barton Airline and the pilot as Lennet. So far her suspicions were proving correct, but where did Walter Baker fit into the picture?

The pilot left the plane with two paper parcels in his arm. Thelma met him on the beach and took the packages from him. Their words were not audible to Beverly, but she watched until Lennet went back to the plane and Thelma took the parcels to her car. Then, before the plane could rise into the air and give the pilot a chance to see her, Beverly ran back to the seclusion of her own car and waited.

As soon as the plane was aloft and winging its way toward the Barton airfield, Thelma started her car and turned toward Miami. Beverly followed at a discreet distance. She wished she knew positively what was in the packages Lennet had given Thelma, but she was confident she could make a close guess. It was time now to call in official help. She clung tenaciously to Thelma's trail until the girl parked her car in front of her house and disappeared within, carrying the brown paper packages with her.

Then Beverly went to see the T-man whose name Charlie Blaine had given her. From now on, it would be up to the authorities.

Mr. Weber, gray-haired and pleasant, looked more like someone's benevolent uncle than an agent for the Treasury Department. He and a young police lieutenant listened attentively as Beverly made a complete report of her discoveries.

"I also found a list of numbers which I think are serial numbers copied from counterfeit currency." Beverly produced her copy of the list she had found by Thelma's desk and of which the girl had at first disclaimed all knowledge. "And I have a counterfeit ten-dollar bill which was received in the mail by Philip Barton," Beverly said, producing the bill. "I think, when you check its serial number with the ones on the counterfeits I found in the hidden plane and mailed in to you, you'll find it belongs in the same series."

When the package arrived in the mail the next day, Beverly proved to be right.

"Mr. Weber, I know it's no part of my job to

make suggestions to the Treasury Department," she said now, hesitantly, "but could you prevent Mr. Barton's stolen plane from being impounded? He has an important shipment to make on Monday, and he needs that plane so badly."

"I think that can be arranged," Mr. Weber assured her. "We will examine the plane on the spot, and unless further evidence turns up, there's no reason why it can't be released."

Mr. Weber rose and shook hands with Beverly cordially. "You have done an excellent job, Miss Gray," he declared heartily. "We are positive of the identity of the head of this band of counterfeiters. He operates out of Chicago, but up to now we have been unable to prove his connection with the ring, because we were unable to locate the point of entry of the money. We shall put Miss Chase under surveillance at once. If, as you suspect, the two packages contain counterfeit money and we can catch her with them in her possession, we can make an arrest. We may need you at a moment's notice. Where can we reach you?"

"At the Chalfont. I'll wait for your call," Beverly promised. "I would like to be in at the finish of this."

"We'll call you as soon as the girl makes another move," Mr. Weber promised. "Then we will go to the Barton airfield and pick up her confederate."

Beverly drove back to the hotel, where she found Larry pacing nervously up and down the lobby.

"I've been frantic with worry!" he exclaimed. "I couldn't imagine what had happened to you when you didn't come back all day, and I couldn't make anything out of your message."

"I'll tell you all about it," Beverly promised. "Come and sit with me while I have my dinner. I'm dying of hunger."

While she relaxed she told Larry about the day's events and added her plans for the next day.

"Philip Barton will need the missing plane tomorrow," Beverly said, "and unless I hear from Mr. Weber to the contrary, there's no reason why you can't fly it right to the field in the morning. I am going to telephone Philip tonight and tell him we found it. He can plan his shipment when he knows about it."

A waiter approached their table with a telephone. Philip Barton was calling to tell Beverly that Lennet had landed safely at the field and everything seemed perfectly normal. Philip had driven back to Miami with him and dropped him at his home. Beverly thanked him and told him about the discovery of his lost plane. For a moment Philip was speechless.

"How did you do it, Beverly? I owe you a debt of gratitude I can never repay. I think I will really make you a partner in the business."

"You may not want to when you hear my whole story," Beverly said. "I am afraid you are going to land in the newspapers again—but the story will be favorable this time."

"If you can restore my plane and save the Allied Farms contract for me I will forgive anything," Philip said. "May I come over to your hotel now to talk with you? I'd like to know how you found the plane—"

Beverly, mindful that Mr. Weber might call her away at any moment, refused swiftly.

"I won't be able to tell you the complete story until morning," Beverly answered. "I'll see you at the field then."

"If you told him everything now, the news of Thelma's difficulties might reach Lennet and he would disappear before the police can get to him," Larry told her, as she hung up.

Beverly and Larry spent an hour in the hotel

lobby waiting in vain for a telephone call from Mr. Weber. It was late when Beverly decided to go to her room.

"I don't believe Thelma will do anything now until tomorrow," she declared. "You have an early date with an airplane, remember? You better get some rest."

"Call me if there's anything I can do," Larry insisted.

Beverly went to her room and lay, fully dressed, across the bed. She wanted to be ready at a moment's notice for anything that might happen. She was tired, but she didn't want to sleep. She thought of her story and what a different ending it might have had. Tomorrow night at this time Charlie Blaine should have the whole thing.

What was Thelma waiting for? Why didn't she act? Beverly didn't like this lull in the proceedings. Had something gone wrong? Had Thelma escaped the T-men's net? Beverly glanced at her small traveling clock standing beside the bed. In the glow from a neon sign outside she could see the hour. So much time had elapsed since she had seen Thelma take the packages into her home!

Perhaps Mr. Weber was not going to live up to

his promise. Perhaps he didn't want a reporter present at the final moment to make note of all the details for a curious public.

Philip Barton was shaken, she knew, by what he finally had realized was transpiring right under his nose. Lennet and Thelma—but what about Walter Baker? Where did he fit into the picture? Was he the power behind the throne, so to speak? Had he locked her in the warehouse to give Thelma, Lennet, and himself time to get safely out of town?

Worries and uncertainties danced through Beverly's mind as she lay and waited in the darkness.

At first she wasn't sure she had heard the knock. When it was repeated she jumped up and snapped on the light, aware that unwittingly she must have fallen asleep.

"Who is it?" she called quietly.

"From Mr. Weber's office," a man's voice replied.

When she opened her door two men confronted her.

"Miss Gray?"

"Yes?"

One of the men showed her his credentials. "Will you come with us, please?"

CHAPTER XVII

The Trap

BEVERLY accompanied the men to a long, dark sedan. Mr. Weber was waiting for her.

"We have learned that Miss Chase has made a reservation on a Chicago plane. We have a warrant to search her baggage, and for this we need your formal identification of her. If we find the counterfeit money in her possession we can act without delay on the evidence you have given us."

"Is she still at home?" Beverly asked.

"No, she is already on her way to the airport. We haven't much time."

The black sedan made excellent speed through the dark streets to the municipal airport. Despite the hour there were a lot of people going about their business in the terminal building. Several planes were on the field, but there was only one on which luggage was being loaded.

"We want you to see her without being seen by her," Mr. Weber told Beverly. "We will wait in the shadows outside the building until the passengers start to board the plane. There is no Thelma Chase on the passenger manifest, so she must be using an assumed name."

Beverly and the Treasury agent waited beyond the pattern of light cast by the door through which the passengers stepped from the terminal building to the field. No one paid them any heed. The work necessary to prepare the big plane for its flight went on as usual. Slowly the passengers began to go aboard. It was drawing close to departure time.

"There she is!" Beverly exclaimed in a tense whisper.

"The blonde girl in the black hat is the one you saw take two paper-wrapped parcels from the pilot who made an unscheduled landing in a Barton airplane today?" Weber questioned in a low voice.

"Yes," Beverly said, with an unexpected twinge of pity, knowing that her reply would be used as evidence against Thelma.

Thelma had emerged from the building and was hurrying to board the plane without looking to the right or left. She stepped into the cabin and disappeared from sight. Mr. Weber and Beverly turned aside. At a signal from Mr. Weber two suitcases were transferred from the luggage truck to the black sedan in which Beverly and the men had come to the airport. There, on the back seat of the car, the bags were opened. Two brown paper packages were found wrapped in a navy blue sweater. The T-man opened them quickly.

"Counterfeit!" Mr. Weber exclaimed in satisfaction. "The serial numbers on them correspond to the ones on the list you found by her desk," he told Beverly after a quick check. "This has been a good night's work!"

"The plane—" Beverly said as the deafening roar of starting motors broke the quiet of the night. "Thelma is on it—"

"She will be arrested at the first stop," Mr. Weber assured her. "She can't get away. Meanwhile, there is the matter of her confederate here. Where do you think we can find him?"

"I don't know where he lives," Beverly answered, "but if he doesn't learn of Thelma's arrest I am sure he will be at the airfield in the morning."

"I will send some men out there at once to wait for him, and I will be there myself in the morning," Mr. Weber decided.

Once back at her hotel, late as it was, Beverly placed a telephone call to Charlie Blaine. Her editor listened closely to Beverly's tale of the counterfeiters and commended her highly on the speed with which she had worked.

"But what about Philip?" Charlie Blaine asked. "Are you sure his troubles are over?"

"Tomorrow he will have his plane returned and will be able to meet his contract," Beverly said. "His business future looks bright."

"Call me after Lennet is arrested and you have all the details," Blaine directed and hung up.

Beverly replaced the telephone slowly and thoughtfully. She had told Blaine Philip's problems were solved. But were they? The matter of the stolen plane did not seem clear to Beverly. She and Larry had decided that Lennet must have stolen the plane to provide a quick means of escape for himself and Thelma, but if that were true, why had Thelma gone on the passenger plane? It must be that the two were so confident of their success that they did not feel the need to use the Barton plane.

There was also the matter of the counterfeit money that she and Larry had found on the stolen plane. She still could not believe Lennet would be careless enough to leave such telltale evidence where anyone might stumble upon it.

And there was Walter Baker.

Beverly was much too excited and keyed up to sleep well, so she was up early in the morning. She changed into a fresh, navy blue sport dress and went down to the hotel's coffee shop. She had coffee and rolls and then went out to her car.

The ocean sparkled in the early-morning light as she turned south toward the Barton field. She would not be making this drive many more times, and when this story was complete she was determined to take some leisure time in which to see and enjoy Florida. She would, she thought with a chuckle, write the girls on the *Susabella* at length about this, her second vacation. She could imagine Lenora's chagrin when she heard of the exciting story Beverly had covered without her assistance. The girls in New York must be wondering, too, what had become of her. Beverly was glad the secrecy was almost at an end.

When she arrived at the airfield she found Philip Barton standing by the door of the office. He hurried to meet her.

"The Treasury men are waiting in my office," he said with a frown. "I hate to believe this about Lennet, Beverly."

"Anyone could have been deceived," Beverly reassured him. "He and Thelma made a good team. He could bring the counterfeit money into the country on your planes and Thelma could cover his trail in the office. Probably the man in gray who followed me and who was arrested was one of the people he used to dispose of the money."

"We'll learn the truth when Lennet gets here," Philip said grimly. Then his face cleared. "Tell me about my stolen plane. Who is bringing it to the airport?"

"The young man who owns the *Red Bird*." Beverly smiled. "He is my fiancé, Larry Owens. I needed his help, so I asked him to come down."

"Your fiancé!" Philip exclaimed. "No wonder you two seemed to get along so well!"

Beverly laughed. "Let's go inside. If Lennet comes we don't want to warn him by a reception committee on the front steps."

The next arrivals at the field were Mr. Weber and two assistants. They came shortly after Beverly and joined the group in Philip's office. Time passed slowly and they began to despair of Lennet's coming.

"He isn't usually so late," Philip declared. "He must be suspicious."

"He couldn't be," Mr. Weber said calmly. "No word about the girl has been given out, and no incoming calls have been received for her on the switchboard at her apartment house. He couldn't know of her arrest."

Fifteen fretful, suspense-filled minutes passed while the group waited.

"There is a car coming down the road now," Beverly warned. "I think—yes, it is Lennet."

The pilot parked his car beside Beverly's in the lot but did not come into the building. Instead, he began to walk toward hangar No. 2.

"Shall we go after him?" one of the T-men asked.

"No," Mr. Weber said. "Out there he might try to escape. Wait until he comes in here."

"I'll call him," Philip said reluctantly. He went to the door and hailed his pilot. "Oh, Lennet! Come in a moment, please!"

Lennet responded with a wave of his hand and turned toward the office. He entered the building and strode with his usual swagger to Philip's office, whistling softly. In the doorway he paused; the whistle died on his lips. He was instantly on guard against the array of faces which confronted him.

"You are under arrest, Lennet," Mr. Weber said. "We know all about your little counterfeit game."

"Thelma—" Lennet murmured.

Mr. Weber nodded. "We took her off the plane early this morning."

Slowly Lennet looked from one to the other, his gaze coming to rest at last upon Beverly, who was nearest to him.

"Maybe you've got Thelma, but you haven't got me!" he cried.

In an instant he whipped a revolver from his pocket and, seizing Beverly, held her in front of him as a shield against the drawn weapons of the officers while he backed slowly from the room.

CHAPTER XVIII

More Trouble

"STAY where you are!"

Lennet acted so swiftly and unexpectedly that for a moment the other people in the room were stunned. When they recovered from their surprise they were still helpless. He menaced them all with his revolver, including the girl he held as shield and hostage.

"If no one moves before I reach my car I will release Miss Gray unharmed," he promised.

"You won't get away," Mr. Weber declared.

"At least I'll have a chance," Lennet replied. "Remember! No one is to follow me—or the girl will suffer for it!"

Beverly was forced to walk between Lennet and the police. They reached the hall and continued to the end of it. The man was desperate and Beverly knew that at the slightest move from anyone, herself included, he would not hesitate to use his gun. Therefore, she was an unwilling but compliant hostage.

When they reached the glass door leading to the field, Lennet paused to glance back over his shoulder. No one had followed them into the hallway. Apparently satisfied, he pushed Beverly out the door ahead of him and started along the path. At the corner of the building a pair of strong arms reached out and seized him.

One of the T-men had climbed out the window of the office and waited for them, concealed by the building.

In another moment Lennet was handcuffed and his career of crime was over. With his capture his bravado left him and he sullenly answered all questions put to him.

Lennet confessed that he had been using his job with the Barton Airline to smuggle in counterfeit money made on a printing press hidden in San Joanna, South America. He never brought the money to the Barton field but always arranged to meet his confederate on the beach and deliver the packages of money to him without witnesses.

has been cleared up and you realize at last that I didn't have anything to do with the counterfeit money." He turned to Lennet. "I am sorry, Hugh, I thought you were my good friend. I suppose, though, I haven't really trusted you since the day you stole my plane and gave me that fancy story about being hijacked."

"I was hijacked," Lennet insisted. "I told the truth about that."

"Didn't you steal it and hide it in order to have a means of making a quick escape?" Beverly asked quickly.

"No," Lennet shook his head. "Has it been found?"

Beverly nodded. "And the counterfeit money was right where you left it."

"I hoped it had crashed and the money had been destroyed," Lennet said. "But if you found the plane, you must realize I didn't hide it. I never would have left the money on it."

"Then who did steal it and why?" Philip demanded.

"I don't know," Lennet said heavily.

Beverly and Philip stood in the doorway and watched the Treasury agents start away with their prisoner. Lennet was just climbing into the long black sedan when Walter Baker appeared.

"Good morning, Mr. Baker," Beverly said with a quiet smile, wondering what he thought when he saw her here instead of locked in an empty warehouse cellar.

"Good morning." Walter was smooth and undisturbed. None of his private feelings showed in his face. "What has happened here, Philip?"

"The T-men finally caught up with some counterfeiters," Philip answered. "Lennet and Thelma, of all people! Come into my office and I'll tell you all about it."

"Counterfeiters!" Baker exclaimed. "What—"

There was a faint drone in the sky, ever increasing in volume. Beverly glanced at her wrist watch and then looked skyward.

"Here comes your plane, Mr. Barton. Right on schedule!"

Three pairs of eyes found the silver speck against the puffs of white cloud in the blue sky and followed its progress.

"Our talk will have to wait, Walter," Philip said. "I want to see my plane and thank the pilot."

"What plane?" Walter asked in surprise. "Did you buy a new one?"

"The plane which was stolen," Philip said over his shoulder. "We have it back and just in time to make our first delivery for Allied Farms. We may yet pull the business out of financial trouble, Walter!"

"It's incredible!" Walter breathed as they stood on the field and watched Larry set the plane down on the runway. "Who found it?"

"Miss Gray and her fiancé," Philip said happily. "I told you it was a lucky day for the Barton Airline when I hired her."

"How is it you knew where to look for it?" Walter wanted to know of Beverly. "I think it is a little odd that you should find the plane when the authorities failed."

"The authorities were looking for a crashed plane," Beverly said calmly. "I was not."

"And why not?" Walter demanded. "Everyone else thought the plane had crashed. It was the natural supposition. Why were you so sure it hadn't? Perhaps you had something to do with its disappearance also!" he added nastily.

"Stop it, Walter!" Philip exclaimed. "Miss Gray is above suspicion. Can't you just be glad we have the plane back in good condition? This may save your job and the life of the company!"

"Mr. Baker doesn't seem at all happy to have his job saved," Beverly commented dryly.

"I have always had the interests of the Barton Airline at heart," Walter replied stiffly.

"This is no time for silly quibbling," Philip put in. "Bury the hatchet, you two!"

Philip turned to the runway as Larry taxied the plane close to them.

"Nothing has ever looked so good to me as that plane does this minute! As soon as I make a little money, Beverly, I am going to give a party for you and your fiancé—the biggest party you have ever seen!"

Philip ran out to meet Larry as the door to the cabin opened. Beverly and Walter waited.

"It is odd," Beverly mused slowly, watching her companion out of the corner of her eye. "We were sure Lennet had stolen the plane for his getaway, but he denied it and I believe him."

"How can you believe a man like that?" Walter shrugged. "You say he is a confessed criminal. Why would he hesitate to lie about the plane?"

"He told the truth about the other things he had done," Beverly countered. "I believe he told the truth about the plane. He had nothing to gain by lying."

"You may believe what you want to," Walter said coldly, turning toward the office. "I have work to do."

Beverly smiled as she watched him go. He was retreating under fire. Then her smile turned into a thoughtful frown. If Walter Baker wasn't connected with the counterfeiters, why had he locked her in the warehouse?

And if Lennet hadn't stolen the plane, who had? That question kept coming back to puzzle her more and more. One thing was certain. Whoever had stolen the plane was the same person who sent the blackmail note to Philip. The serial number on the bill enclosed proved that.

There was still an enemy somewhere, and Barton Airline would not be safe until he was discovered and dragged out into the open. She had thought she could go home, once the counterfeiters were discovered, but that was not so. Charlie Blaine wanted young Philip Barton to be helped as much as possible. Philip and his business would not be safe as long as the person who had stolen the plane was unknown and still in a position to do him harm.

CHAPTER XIX

Stowaway

As THE morning progressed, preparations were completed for the first shipment for Allied Farms. Philip explained Larry's duties to him and confided again how important it was that this first assignment under the new contract be accomplished smoothly.

Beverly tried to keep a watchful eye on all the preparations. Philip was too happy at having his plane restored to suspect that there might be more trouble, but Beverly was almost sure there would be. If only she knew from what quarter it would come!

Beverly was on her way to Philip's office when she overheard Walter Baker and Larry talking.

"I think you are simply wasting your time,"

Walter was saying. "The Barton Airline is washed up. Barton doesn't realize that not even the contract with Allied Farms can save it."

"What do you mean?" Larry asked innocently.

"I mean, you won't even collect your salary," Baker replied. "If I were you I would go get a job with one of the other lines."

"I promised Mr. Barton to fly his plane to New Orleans and back," Larry protested. "It wouldn't be fair to him. He is depending upon me."

"It won't be fair to you either, when you don't get paid for your work," Walter pointed out. "I'm giving you some good advice. Barton Airline is going to collapse and you are likely to be stranded without a job or money."

"If what you say is true," Larry frowned, still feigning innocence, "how did Mr. Barton get the contract with Allied Farms?"

"I suspect it was simply because his father is John K. Barton," Walter replied angrily. "However, he won't have the contract very long—or the airline either."

"Just the same, I think I'll take this flight out for him," Larry said and walked away.

"Fool!" Walter muttered. "At least I warned him!"

Walter stalked back to his desk and Beverly, staring out across the flying field, suddenly realized the big mistake she had made. She had confidently believed that all the trouble on the Barton Airline came from the counterfeiters. She had assumed that Lennet and Thelma stole the plane, that they wrote the mysterious note which had drawn Philip and herself away from the field, that it was they who for some inexplicable reason had been trying to ruin Philip's business. She had been right in everything but the last supposition. It had been and still was *Walter Baker* who wanted to stab Philip in the back. She knew that it was Walter who had damaged the plane the day she saw him sneaking out of the hangar. It must have been someone working for Walter who stole the plane from Lennet. And it was Walter who had tried to frighten Philip off with the threatening letter and the incriminating counterfeit bill—just as he had tried to scare her with the crude warnings.

So far, all of Walter's tricks had failed. It seemed that, in spite of all Walter had done, young Philip Barton was on the verge of success. Beverly felt confident that Walter would try again, desperately now, to wreak what havoc he could. She was sure, too, after overhearing the conversation with Larry, that Walter's next attempt would come on the flight to New Orleans. It was Walter's last chance to accomplish his strange objective.

Beverly hurried out to the plane where Larry was talking to Joe, who was putting gasoline into the ship.

"Hi," Larry said. "Want to go flying with me into the wild blue yonder?"

"No, and I don't want you to, either," Beverly replied, frowning.

"Don't look so worried," Larry said, surprised, as he joined her. "It isn't much of a trip."

"It might amount to more than you think," Beverly said. "Larry, I want you to give it up. Don't go! Tell Philip you have suddenly been called back to New York. I don't want you to fly for the Barton line. Please, Larry!"

"What?" Larry gasped. "You got me down here to fill in this spot, didn't you?"

"That was before the counterfeiters were caught," Beverly said hurriedly. "Now I have changed my mind. Don't take this flight out, Larry."

"What has gotten into you?" Larry demanded. "Oh-ho! I'll bet I know what it is! My, what big ears you've got, grandma!"

"All right," Beverly said, smiling, "maybe I did overhear you and Walter Baker. I know a warning when I hear one, too, and he warned you!"

"He gave me advice," Larry corrected.

"Something will happen on this trip, I know it will!" Beverly insisted.

"Nothing is going to happen." Larry tried to calm her. "It is a fine ship and in tiptop condition. I'll be there and back before you know it." He took her by the shoulders and shook her gently. "Come on, Bev, throw away that frown. Don't let any little gremlins scare you. Walter's bark is worse than his bite, believe me."

"Can't you see, Larry, that he is the one who has been behind all the trouble here? Now he intends to make one last effort to wreck the line for Philip."

"All the more reason to put our shoulders to the wheel for dear old Barton Airline," Larry chuckled reassuringly.

"Larry, give up this trip—for me," Beverly pleaded.

"I can't, Bev," Larry said. "I promised Philip to see it through. You wouldn't want me to break my promise, would you?"

Beverly made no reply.

"I take off in fifteen minutes," Larry said,

consulting his watch. "I'd better go in now and pick up my charts. We have a date with the best dinner in town as soon as I get back."

"But Larry—" Beverly made one more attempt to stop him.

"I'll go get the charts and be right back," Larry said. "Wait for me by the plane."

Beverly watched him go toward the office. At a window of the building Walter Baker was watching, too. If only Larry would believe her and refuse to take the plane off the ground! If anything happened aboard the plane—anything to hurt Larry—Beverly would never forgive herself. She had drawn him into this tangled web of mystery. She wished now that he had stayed safely in New York.

Besides, this was her assignment. She had given her promise, too, to see the thing through to the end. It wasn't fair now to pass the ending on to Larry. She wanted to be present at the final blow, but if it took place on the plane that would not be possible.

Beverly looked up as the mechanic started warming the big motors. She firmly believed that the last act of the drama would be played in the cabin of the plane. If she wanted to be a participant, what was she waiting for?

A glance around told her that Larry had not yet emerged from the office. The mechanic was too busy to notice her. Beverly swung herself up into the cabin, smiling to herself as she thought of how amazed Larry would be when he found he had a stowaway on board.

CHAPTER XX

The Culprit

BEVERLY found a hiding place in the cargo compartment among the crates and boxes and settled herself for the flight. She could not be seen by anyone entering the plane, so she felt that she would be safe from discovery until she chose to reveal her presence after they were airborne. She had barely gotten settled when she heard a noise close to her and realized that someone else had boarded the plane. Thinking it was the mechanic making sure the cargo was secure, she remained stiff and silent, on the alert, but no one discovered her.

A short time later she heard voices and Larry and Philip Barton climbed into the cabin.

"As I said to Walter, Owens," Philip was saying, "it is not my policy to go along on freight deliveries, and it's no reflection on you, but something tells me this flight is going to be the turning point in my career. I want to make it with you."

"Several people have had a hunch about this trip," Larry responded, chuckling.

"I wish I had told Beverly I was going along," Philip continued. "Susan might telephone and worry when I am not to be found."

"When Beverly can't find you on the field, I believe she will guess where you have gone," Larry told him. "It is odd where she disappeared to. She was going to wait for me by the plane."

Their voices blurred as they went up into the cockpit and Beverly settled herself for the take-off.

The motors increased their roar. The plane vibrated and shook as it began to move down the runway. It was a smooth take-off as the great wings lifted the plane into the air. The earth fell away below them, a checkerboard pattern of brown and green.

Beverly sat without stirring. If Philip discovered her presence this early in the trip he might turn back and insist upon leaving her at the field. She decided that she would wait until they were well under way before she revealed herself to the two men up front.

It was dull, sitting on the floor between the boxes of cargo. She could not see out any window, and could only guess at what was passing below. From time to time she heard the murmur of Larry's and Philip's voices, but she could not distinguish the words.

A half-hour passed on her watch and she was beginning to think that she had been unduly alarmed. The trip had been smooth and peaceful so far. She decided to wait another fifteen minutes and then go up to the pilot's seat and announce her presence. She smiled to herself as she thought of the amazement of the two young men. Tonight the three of them could dine in New Orleans and tomorrow they would fly back to Miami. She was glad her premonition of evil events had not been fulfilled.

Beverly stood up and smoothed the wrinkles out of her skirt. She stepped out of her hiding place and then suddenly drew back. A man's head and shoulders were slowly appearing from behind a crate in front of her. His back was to her and he was approaching the door to the pilot's compartment. The plane had two stowaways and the second was Walter Baker!

Beverly crouched down out of sight and waited to see what would happen. She hadn't long to wait. The plane lurched so suddenly that she was thrown off balance to the floor. At the same time she heard Philip's voice rise in surprise.

"Walter! What are you doing here?"

"Surprised, Philip?"

Beverly scrambled up and stole closer to the cockpit to hear what was going on. The scene there was so tense that no one noticed her.

"What are you doing here—and with that gun?" Philip demanded again.

"This is to persuade your pilot to follow my orders," Walter replied smoothly. "Change your course to due east," he directed.

"My course is southwest," Larry replied calmly. "I do not intend to change it."

"I think you will," Walter said. "I have come too far to let anyone stop me now. We fly east—over the ocean."

"Why?" Philip demanded.

"You and Mr. Owens are going to get out," Walter answered.

"Are you mad?" Philip gasped. "How would you get back? You're not a pilot. And even if you did manage to get back, how would you explain our disappearance?"

"I've gone to a lot of trouble to get control of Barton Airline legally," Walter said swiftly. "Now it's time for sterner measures. I have been flying a plane for years," he continued; "and there will be a satisfactory explanation of your—shall we say 'accident'? After all, a plane in flight is no place for the pilot to start an argument with the man who is paying too much attention to the pilot's fiancée. It's apt to lead to violence and—tragedy."

Beverly had been listening white-faced. So that was it! This madman—for surely Walter Baker must be insane—was going to attempt to convince the authorities that Larry and Philip, arguing over *her*, had gone to their deaths in the Atlantic Ocean! He would never get away with it, she knew, shuddering, but that wouldn't bring Larry and Philip back.

"But *why*, man?" she heard Larry ask. "Why commit murder for the sake of getting control of a freight airline that at best will never make you rich?"

"That depends on the cargo you carry," Walter Baker returned. His tone changed suddenly. "Alter your course, Mr. Owens, as I directed, and do it now!"

"Better do as he says," Philip told Larry reluctantly.

"Sit still!" Walter's voice whipped out the command. "Heroics would be useless."

Beverly held her breath. Larry must have started to protest the man's demands. She could feel the plane changing course. What Walter proposed was incredible. He talked calmly of dropping both Larry and Philip from the plane as if it were of no consequence.

"East, Mr. Owens!" Walter's voice reminded the pilot. "Don't try any tricks!"

"I thought you were my friend, Walter," Philip began slowly. "Why? Why are you doing this?"

"That is my business," Walter snapped. "You don't know anything about business." His voice was scornful. "It was simple to reduce the line to nothing until I chose to save it. From now on, it will be the Baker Airline. Stay on your new course, Mr. Owens!"

All the admonitions to Larry worried Beverly. She knew he would not submit lightly to Walter's commands.

"Reduce the air speed," Walter continued. "Barton, you will go first."

"What is it you want, Walter?" Philip persisted. "Is it necessary to kill us—"

"There have been too many setbacks to my

plans in the past," Walter answered. "This time I am going to make sure I get the line."

"You won't get away with this!" Larry exclaimed. He suddenly caught sight of Beverly, and just for an instant there was a flicker of surprise in his eyes.

"I think I will," Walter said confidently. "My plans have been well laid. It will—"

His words ended abruptly as he whirled around to face Beverly, who stood in the doorway behind him.

"You again!" Baker snarled, and raised his gun just as Larry and Philip tackled him.

There was one shot and Beverly saw Philip Barton slump to the floor, blood gushing from a wound in his arm. The plane, with no one at the controls, lurched dangerously and started into a spin.

CHAPTER XXI

End of the Jinx

WHILE Larry and Walter Baker struggled for possession of the revolver, Beverly managed to reach the pilot's seat. She was deeply grateful now for her pilot's training. Their survival depended on her, and slowly but surely she was able to pull the plane out of its twisting fall and level it off before it reached the green sea water.

There was a grunt and a groan behind her, and when she looked around Walter lay motionless on the floor and Larry was holding the revolver.

"He's out cold," Larry said. "Get the first-aid kit, Bev, and see what you can do for Barton. I'll head the plane back to the field."

Larry radioed Joe Dean at the field that they were turning back and told him to have the police waiting for them when they landed.

"That will put an end to his little game," Philip said with satisfaction. He grimaced as Beverly swabbed the blood from his arm and bandaged it.

"It is only a flesh wound," she said in relief. "The bullet never touched the bone. You will be all right in a short time."

"He is right enough now to hold this gun on Baker," Larry said, grinning, and pressed the revolver into Philip's good hand. Baker had regained consciousness and was trying to sit up.

"It would give me great pleasure to use it on him," Philip declared angrily.

Walter glowered at the three of them from his position on the floor.

"I might use it, too," Philip continued, "unless he tells me what I want to know."

"You wouldn't dare," Walter gritted. "You've never had the nerve to do anything without your father's help."

Philip's face reddened.

"I might have been like that once, but lately I've been learning to stand on my own feet." He gripped the revolver with new determination. "I want to know why you've been determined to ruin me."

Walter was silent and Philip glanced at Larry. The latter winked at Beverly.

"If he won't talk, Philip, we could dump him into the ocean as he proposed to do to us," Larry said blandly.

"You couldn't get away with it," Walter retorted.

"I think we could," Larry continued. "You stowed away on the plane. No one knows you are here. You wouldn't be traced to us."

Walter was silent, his gaze traveling from one silent young face to the next.

"Why have you done all these things to me?" Philip demanded again.

"I knew you wouldn't sell, so I tried to drive you out of business and buy the airline at my own price," Walter said sulkily. "I almost succeeded, too."

"Did you want to smuggle in counterfeit money?" Philip asked in surprise. "Were you in league with Lennet after all?"

"I had nothing to do with Lennet or Thelma," Walter denied. "I suspected Lennet, but I never found out that Thelma was working with him."

"It is my guess you planned to use the airplanes to smuggle in human cargo," Larry put in shrewdly.

"How did you—" Walter burst out, then broke off, realizing he had confirmed Larry's suspicion.

"Aliens?" Beverly asked.

Larry nodded. "There are certain undesirable characters who will pay any price for transportation into this country unknown to the Bureau of Immigration. I have had a hunch that was it, ever since we saw Baker on the *Mary B*."

"Then it was you two the sailor surprised on deck that night!" Walter said in astonishment.

"I didn't believe your story about a week end of fishing," Beverly told him. "Why did you lock me in the warehouse yesterday?"

"I knew you were suspicious of me. I was meeting someone in town and I had to get rid of you," Walter retorted, "so I deliberately led you to the warehouse."

"And you're the one who's been warning me to leave the Barton line," Beverly continued.

Walter nodded sullenly. "Since the day you arrived I suspected you of watching me secretly."

"But why did you ask Philip for five thousand dollars when you knew he didn't have it?" Beverly pressed.

"I knew he didn't have five cents," Walter sneered. "And I didn't expect him to have nerve enough to go to Heyman's Swamp. The threatening letter was just an excuse to send him one of the counterfeit bills we found in the plane after one of my men hijacked it. I was going to tip off the T-men to come and search Barton's office for counterfeit. That would have cooked his goose."

"What a lot you'll have to answer for when we hand you over to the police!" Philip told Walter in disgust.

"And what a story I'll have for the paper," Beverly added. "This is one story your father will be happy to read, Philip. You are a hero! If you and Larry hadn't gotten that gun away from Walter we might all be at the bottom of the ocean by now."

When the plane landed on the Barton field the police were on hand and so was Susan Trent.

"Philip!"

"I'm all right, Sue," Philip told her soothingly, "and it is the end of our jinx."

As soon as the police took charge of Walter Baker, Beverly telephoned Charlie Blaine the complete details. She praised Philip highly, and that seemed to please her editor.

"You've done a fine job, Beverly," Blaine declared. "Thank you. Your old job is waiting for you—with a raise in salary."

Beverly went happily out to confide in Larry

and Philip. They were discussing the problem of the freight shipments.

"My trouble with Walter Baker is over, but I still have my contract to meet," Philip said ruefully.

"I'll take off immediately," Larry promised. "I'll return tomorrow morning and Wednesday I will make another delivery for you. I'll fly for Barton Airline until you have time to hire some new pilots."

Larry was true to his word. He made the first delivery in record time and without incident. He radioed when he would return, and Philip and Beverly were on hand to welcome him.

"I can't ever thank you and Larry, Beverly," Philip said as they waited on the field for Larry. "Susan and I owe our future to you."

"Don't say that, Phil," Beverly said, smiling. "You're going to make a happy future for yourselves."

"I like the idea of making it myself." Philip grinned. "I wish my father could see me now. The proudest day of my life will be the day he knows I am a success because of my own efforts."

A tiny speck appeared on the horizon and they watched it grow in size as it neared the airport.

"That isn't Larry," Beverly said, puzzled.

"Were you expecting any other plane to land here?"

"I haven't received word that any would," Philip answered. "It is a small craft—something like the *Red Bird*. I wonder—" He broke off, shading his eyes with his hand as the plane passed in front of the sun. "It is the *Challenger*—my father's private plane!"

"Maybe he wants to meet Susan," Beverly smiled.

"He doesn't know about her—yet," Philip said. "If he has come to fight with me about that newspaper story—"

"Knock that chip off your shoulder," Beverly chuckled. "It isn't becoming. Smile—you'll find it's contagious."

Unwillingly at first, Philip's face broke into a smile as they walked toward the plane coming down the runway. As soon as the door to the cabin opened, a portly gentleman in a gray business suit stepped out and strode toward Philip.

"Phil, my boy!"

Tactfully Beverly turned from the reunion of father and son to welcome a second visitor.

"Charlie Blaine!" she exclaimed. "What are you doing here?"

"John made me come along," her editor

grinned. "He could hardly wait to see the boy. He was worried about his wounded arm, I expect."

"It isn't serious," Beverly assured him.

Blaine chuckled. "Poor Philip looks a little overwhelmed by his father's solicitude. I suppose you know all is forgiven."

"It should be," Beverly said. "Philip is a nice boy."

"He can thank you for changing his father's attitude," Blaine declared. "You did a first-rate job all around, Beverly. By the way, I have another story I want you to go after. Can you start at once?"

"The *Tribune* is a hard taskmaster," Beverly answered. "What is it this time?"

But even while Blaine outlined the course of her future actions, there was a message en route to Beverly which would prevent her return to New York and which would send her on a wholly unexpected and daring venture.

What has become of the "Susabella's" passengers? Seeking her missing friends, Beverly finds herself unexpectedly involved in a dangerous plot. How she assumes an amazing disguise to accomplish an exciting rescue is told in the thrilling story of **BEVERLY GRAY'S MASQUERADE.**